*Linn could feel the heat from his body*

When he moved the hooks of her dress aside and she felt the waistband loosen, goose bumps tiptoed from her waist to her shoulder.

"I know you're not cold," Kellan whispered behind her. "It's seventy-five degrees outside. I'm still waiting for your answer."

"You know how I feel about you."

"I want to hear it."

He slipped the dress off her shoulders. "I can't resist you," she confessed. "I should, but I can't." The red silk whispered down her legs.

"Who says you should? Work is a long way away. There's no one here but us."

When she turned to him, she was naked except for her panties. Her gaze traveled up his trousers and paused on the ridge of his erection under the fine wool.

"This isn't fair. You have more clothes on than I do."

In seconds he'd taken care of that little problem....

# Blaze™

Dear Reader,

These days, having a relationship with someone you work with is fairly common. I married my boss, so I consider myself an authority on the subject! But in the law enforcement community, having a relationship on the job can be a difficult and sometimes dangerous thing. Then again, when you really want something, the rewards are often worth the risks, aren't they? When writing Linn and Kellan's story, I used a lot of my own experience from the years when I worked as support staff for law enforcement. For instance, the opening scene in the glass interrogation room was based on the undercover calls I was often directed to make.

I'm thrilled to be part of the Blaze line, joining authors whose work I've read for years. It's a chance for me to push my own envelope as well as that of romance fiction. Come visit me at www.shannonhollis.com, learn about my book plans and meet the cover model who was the inspiration for Kellan Black!

Warmly,

*Shannon Hollis*

## Books by Shannon Hollis

HARLEQUIN TEMPTATION
931—HER PRIVATE EYE

# HIS HOT NUMBER

*Shannon Hollis*

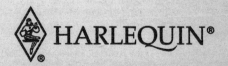

# HARLEQUIN®

TORONTO • NEW YORK • LONDON
AMSTERDAM • PARIS • SYDNEY • HAMBURG
STOCKHOLM • ATHENS • TOKYO • MILAN • MADRID
PRAGUE • WARSAW • BUDAPEST • AUCKLAND

For Jeff, with love

Acknowledgments

I'd like to thank the female police officers and FBI agents who so generously
lent me their time and expertise but who, for the sake of their investigations,
declined to be named. Thanks also go to Karolyn, Jenny and Mara for
careful reading and good suggestions, and as always, to my editor,
Jennifer Green, for her hard work and keen eye.

ISBN 0-373-79148-8

HIS HOT NUMBER

Copyright © 2004 by Shelley Bates.

www.eHarlequin.com

Printed in U.S.A.

# 1

JUST HER LUCK—she was a phone-sex virgin.

State investigator Linn Nichols sat alone in a modified glass-walled interrogation room that contained the secure phone line nicknamed the "hot number." The undercover investigators always had their targets call that line, whose number was changed for every new operation. It was always answered by someone who had been briefed on what to say, and the conversations were always recorded.

Half a dozen men stood at the windows watching her, probably already planning how they were going to tell the guys on swing shift about this when they got in. It wasn't every day that a female investigator transferred into the narcotics division of the California Law Enforcement Unit, much less one who had agreed to give them this kind of entertainment on a Wednesday morning.

She might have earned her stripes with the covert ops unit of the Santa Rita PD, but she was an unknown entity to these guys. Too bad she couldn't have proved herself in some other way.

She couldn't think about her audience. Right now

it was just Linn and Rick O'Reilly, the West Coast's slipperiest cocaine importer, on the phone, all alone.

All she had to do was make him believe.

No problem. "Fake it till you make it." That was the mantra in narcotics. If she wasn't exactly sure how to fake a seduction over the phone, she'd figure it out in the next ten minutes, or die of embarrassment trying.

The tallest of the men who were ranged along the glass nudged the guy beside him without taking his eyes off her. She was only a rookie with a grand total of one State of California paycheck to her credit, which was probably why she hadn't seen him before. Unlike the others, he didn't wear an identification badge on a clip. He couldn't be a civilian, though—he had too good a rapport with the other investigators. And he definitely wasn't a lawyer. With the confident stance of someone who had taken on the worst the streets had to offer—and beaten it—he shook back the hair that brushed his shoulders.

And what shoulders they were, too. The black Aerosmith concert T-shirt stretched tight across his chest and wrapped around upper arms hard with muscle. The T-shirt was tucked into a pair of worn jeans that hugged him and invited a woman to stroke him where the fabric was faded and soft at his hip, thigh and fly.

With a start she realized she was staring at his crotch, and worse, he'd caught her at it. One corner of his mouth lifted in a half grin.

That did it. Linn focused on the scratched wood

tabletop and tried to channel her energy into making up a character. It wasn't that she could feel him watching her, or that she couldn't drag in enough oxygen to stop the erratic pounding of her heart, or that, despite her jacket and jeans, she was freezing.

She had to do this right. The team was counting on her to get them the information they needed, and she couldn't let some buff biker type and his nudging and smiling distract her.

When the phone rang, Nudge-and-Smile shifted his weight to the other foot. She took a deep breath and put her head down on her arm along the tabletop. She'd heard once that the differing tensions on the throat changed the sound of the voice when the body was horizontal. She hoped it was true. She needed to sound tousled and sleepy—a woman ripe for pillow talk.

Allowing her lips to soften into a pout, Linn relaxed her shoulders and picked up the receiver.

"Hello?" Her voice was a seductive whisper, as if she'd been awakened by the phone. Out of the corner of her eye, she saw the operator give the thumbs-up, and the men leaned in to listen to the recording equipment outside the room. Nudge-and-smile crossed his arms and narrowed his gaze.

There was a pause while the suspect on the other end of the line adjusted. He hadn't been expecting her. The call had been set up between him and an operative known on the streets as "Dean," a guy whose identity was so secret Linn didn't yet know which of the investigators he was.

"Well, hi. Who's this?"

"Caroline." Linn injected the rounded vowels of Kensington W8 into her voice, gleaned from an exchange term spent at Oxford studying the history of justice administration. "And who is this?"

"Rick. Dean didn't tell me about any Carolines. Now I know why."

"Oh?" she purred, as if she already knew the answer, as if men were in the habit of keeping her their dirty little secret.

"Because he knows what a sucker I am for a pretty voice."

"Don't you mean face?" *You scumball charmer, you.*

"Voice for now. Face, maybe later. Like when Dean lets you out in public so I can buy you a drink."

"There is no *let*. If I want to have a drink with you, darling, I will."

"You shouldn't talk to strangers that way."

"You're no stranger…Richard."

Suspicion leaked into his voice. "How come I haven't met you?"

She was going to have to tread carefully here, while doing her best to sound ingenuous. "I only arrived this week."

"Dean never said anything."

"Does he share his love life with you? Oooh, I'm either going to have to be very, very careful or very, very bad. Which would you prefer?"

She'd taken him aback a second time, judging by his pause. Hard to believe when you considered the element he hung around with.

She glanced up and locked gazes with nudge-and-smile. Why was he staring at her as if she were a lock and he had a handful of picks?

"I like a bad girl who's very, very careful."

Rick's voice sounded in her ear—and on the tape—and she dragged her attention back to him. "I'm always careful. So much so that you probably don't know we have a mutual friend."

"Yeah?"

"Hidalgo Martinez sends his regards from Acapulco. He has a new house there. I visited last winter."

"No kidding." He stopped. "Was that before or after he got busted?"

"Before, unfortunately." She sighed with regret. "It was *such* a lovely house."

But if O'Reilly contacted Martinez, who had been one of his distributors and was out on bail in Miami while he waited for his trial, he'd find that Martinez would corroborate her story. He'd "flipped" and given CLEU a ton of information—not to mention agreed to back up her cover story—in exchange for a reduction in his charges.

"Thanks for the message. Hidalgo's a good guy."

"Dean's told me you are, too."

"Oh, yeah? What did he say?"

She stretched a little more, giving herself a moment to synthesize the information in the case file into something she could use for an answer. "Oh, just that you're one of the smart ones who can do business without bringing a lot of attention to yourself. Unlike poor Hidalgo."

In other words, Rick O'Reilly had managed to weasel out of so many charges that they called him "Tricky Ricky." It helped that he had one of the best defense attorneys in the State on his payroll, and for all they knew, a couple of deputy D.A.s, as well.

"Dean said that?" He sounded pleased. Was Dean's opinion important to him in some way? Or was it merely the competitive posturing of a pair of alpha males? Linn wished she knew more. She filed the information in the Rolodex in her brain in case she needed it later.

"Absolutely. But you should ask him, not me."

"I can think of other things to ask you. Like where you are right now, pretty lady. And what you're wearing."

Oh, God, the guy was a walking, talking cliché. "What makes you suppose I'm wearing anything?"

"Are you?"

"Yes." She pretended disappointment at having to confess it. "A little Dior camisole I picked up the last time I was in Paris. Silk."

"What color?"

"Red."

"Does Dean like it?"

"He likes me better without it."

"I bet I would, too. What are you doing Saturday night?"

"Mmm." She stretched along the table, like a woman reluctant to get out of bed. "Why don't I call you back when I'm decent and I know I'm alone?"

"I like you indecent. Take off the cami-thing. Touch yourself. Tell me what it feels like."

"Bad boy."

"I can be very bad. Come on. Take it off. We can be bad together."

The giggle felt foreign in her throat. "How bad?"

She practically sensed his chest swelling over the line, and resisted the urge to roll her eyes in case he detected the contempt in her voice.

"What if I told you I could give you the baddest night of your life? Not just now, but later. When I've got you all alone."

*Do not groan. Do not even think about laughing.* To lose the urge to giggle, she glanced at the window again. Nudge-and-smile hadn't moved. In fact, now he leaned on the glass with one shoulder, arms still crossed, as if he were trying to get as close to her as he could without actually falling into the room. His head was tilted down a little, and he watched her with half-closed eyes. The heat in his expression intensified, and their gazes locked a second time.

"Tell me more." She wasn't sure if she was talking to O'Reilly or the man at the window. In fact, she could no longer remember what she'd been saying to the dealer.

That was bad. She had to pull it together.

"How about a bottle of Glenlivet, a king-size bed and the hottest sex you've ever had?"

"I've had some pretty hot sex, darling." She said the words to the stranger behind the glass. His shoulders stiffened, and he blinked. She felt mesmerized by that gaze, oddly split between the real man she could see and the one she could only hear.

"Not like this. How about I throw in some spectacular blow? I've got good connections and I'm more than willing to share."

"Ooh, now that changes everything." She hardly knew what she was saying. "I could be talked into a blow of a different sort for that kind of fun."

"Yeah? You are a bad girl. But I forgive you. You do me, I do you, and then we'll do the blow together."

*What?* She broke eye contact with the man at the window, whose jaw had gone slack. Here she was on her maiden voyage into the world of phone sex with not one man, but two. How weird was that? She needed to get things back on track in a hurry, before this went any further and her hard-won reputation as a professional and a fine investigator went down faster than a ten-dollar trick.

"Do you know," she murmured, "Dean will be back any minute, and I'd rather he didn't listen in on my calls." She paused. "Damn. This call was for him, wasn't it?"

"It's yours now, baby. Just like me. I'll meet you at the Dominion Hotel bar on Saturday. Nine o'clock. Wear something red on top of that cami-thing. I like red on bad girls."

"Bother," she sighed. "That means I'll have to lose Dean. On a Saturday night it won't be easy. Give me your number, darling, in case I can't change my plans."

She held her breath. Here was the whole reason she'd been directed to make this call. Good thing she'd remembered to do it.

He dictated it, and through the window, she watched her lieutenant pump his fist in the air in victory as the recording specialist contacted the phone company. Tricky Ricky used disposable cell phones and changed them every few days—one of the reasons CLEU had resorted to using a live investigator to get his number. Time to wind it up.

"I've got to go. I just heard Dean's car. I'll call you."

"I'll be waiting, sweet Caroline."

She dropped the receiver into its cradle and sat up, smoothing her dark hair into its easy-care French braid.

At least the members of her team were no longer standing at the glass like johns at a peep show. They were making notes and huddling, getting ready for a fast trip to O'Reilly's location, which they suspected was his safe house. Because of their joint-forces agreement with the phone company, whose state-of-the-art "E911" emergency tracking system could give them O'Reilly's location within about fifty feet, once they had a number to work with, they no longer had to rely on inaccurate triangulation methods or even old-fashioned surveillance.

For a while, at least, technology had put them one step ahead of the bad guys.

Lieutenant Bryan pushed open the door and let in

a welcome draft of fresh air. His navy ball cap said Get a CLEU in gold embroidery on the front. He pulled it off and fanned his face with it.

"Good work, Nichols. The team ought to be able to pick him up this afternoon." The lieutenant assessed her and rammed the cap back on. "There's more to you than meets the eye, isn't there? That English accent thing was great."

Did he mean she looked as if she weren't capable of being sexy? She'd like to see him try a day as a woman in what most of the investigators still believed was a man's profession. It was dangerous; she wasn't denying that. And the targets rarely, if ever, dealt with women, which was why there weren't many female investigators. If she went a little overboard with the businesslike, cool exterior in the office, it was because she'd learned the hard way that it was best to start out looking as if you had the upper hand.

Sometimes you even got it.

"Picking him up is the plan," the lieutenant went on briskly, "but if he gives us the slip, you've got his confidence. Stupid."

For a second Linn thought Bryan meant her, and she stiffened.

"What kind of a wing nut would come right out and offer to meet a complete stranger? He's either dumb as a box of rocks or has way too much self-confidence." He shook his head and touched her shoulder. "Come on. I'm going to introduce you to the investigator heading up this case."

She followed him out of the glass room. Wasn't

Cooper Maxwell heading up the case? She'd been doing surveillance at his direction for the last week, and he'd been the one to assign the call to her.

The investigators on the heroin and crack teams had scattered to their workstations in the bullpen now that the day's show appeared to be over. As Bryan led her deeper into the cubicles, she saw nudge-and-smile hanging over a fabric-covered divider with both arms crossed on top of it, telling someone on the other side a story that involved him pointing the fingers of one hand like a pistol.

Bryan was leading her straight to him.

This was the case lead? She was going to have to take orders from a man who was not only oozing testosterone all over the cube, but the one to whom she'd just offered a blow job by proxy?

She'd really done it. This man was technically her manager, and what kind of first impression would he have of her now? Every time he gave her an order or an assignment, he'd remember her stretched out and horizontal, propositioning a criminal. And she'd remember hot eyes and soft denim. They would hardly be able to say "good morning" to each other without thinking about sex.

A fine way to start a working relationship.

"Black, meet our newest recruit. Linn Nichols, this is Investigator Kellan Black, known to the criminal underworld as Dean."

KELL LOOKED DOWN at the woman who had just seduced Rick O'Reilly into revealing not only his current phone number, but gotten a few hints about his source, as well. If he hadn't watched her in action himself, he'd never have believed it possible. She'd morphed from a degenerate sex goddess back into a tight-lipped Linda Fiorentino, and was now giving him the once-over as coolly as if she hadn't all but made him—or was it O'Reilly?—an offer he couldn't refuse only moments before.

"Hello." He extended a hand and took hers. Cool fingers. Naturally. She probably had a body temperature of eighty degrees. "Nice work in there."

"Thanks," she said without a trace of that husky purr. He was having a hard time reconciling the sex kitten who had stretched out along the table as if she were about to climb all over a man's body with this unflappable-looking woman in a standard-issue navy jacket, white T-shirt, and jeans so clean they probably hadn't seen the street yet. Her dark-brown hair was pulled back into some kind of braid, but fine wisps blew gently in the gale of the air-conditioning vent above his cubicle. She met his eyes and waited for him to speak.

Her eyes were spectacular, huge and blue and long-lashed. With a little makeup, those eyes could belong to the voice he'd heard on the tape. But he had a feeling makeup was as foreign to her skin as seduction was to her voice.

Or maybe she had multiple personalities and had somehow managed to sneak past the psych screen and the background checks.

"I've got a meeting to get to," the lieutenant said.

"I've told Linn here you're heading up the case. Come up with a game plan in case something goes wrong this afternoon." He hustled out, perpetually overcommitted, leaving Kellan with the woman and no idea where to start.

"Have a seat." He indicated a chair in the corner of the cubicle, next to a coat tree he never used. "How long have you been with us?"

She sat slowly, her back ramrod straight. "A little over three weeks." So that meant she had five months to go in her probationary period. Some of the rookies didn't even last that long.

"Look, Investigator—" she began.

"Kellan. Kell if you're in a hurry. Black if you're mad at me, which the lieutenant sometimes is. And Dean if you're in the market for coke, or out working with me." He tried on a grin, just to see if she'd loosen up, but she didn't.

"Kellan." She said his name with precision, no chummy abbreviations, with the barest trace of some kind of accent on the *e*. He wondered where *that* had come from. Then again, a few minutes ago he would have bet hard cash that she was British. A very posh Brit, used to winter holidays on the Mexican Riviera with drug kingpins who owned lovely houses.

"I need to explain something."

He'd known her for less than thirty seconds. What needed explaining? Well, except maybe for—

"I don't want you to think that my performance in there was my typical method of operation."

He grinned. So he'd been right. "I should be so lucky."

If he expected an answering smile and a little on-the-job camaraderie, he was wrong. Her eyes turned cold. Briefly he wondered what it would take to heat them up to the temperature they'd been when she was on the phone. She was either one hell of an actress or Tricky Ricky had managed to turn her on.

*Don't even go there.*

"This isn't a joke, Kellan. I expect to be treated the way you'd treat any member of your team, and I don't want any fallout from the guys because of the activities I'm directed to perform."

He slumped in his swivel chair and regarded her with a frown, resolutely slapping away a mental list of several activities he might perform with the woman in the glass room. Who definitely was not the woman who sat in front of him now and who was making that fact painfully clear.

"You think I'm going to treat you like a slut because you can act like one?"

She actually winced. Maybe there was a little stiff-upper-lip Brit in there after all.

"I'd prefer to avoid that."

"I think you underestimate me. You're a damned fine actress. You got Tricky Ricky on tape admitting to possession with intent to distribute. You practically had him masturbating in under three minutes, so I have nothing but admiration for your skills."

She got up, planted both hands flat on his desk and leaned over him. Heroically, he tried to resist sneaking a peek at her breasts as they swelled in his immediate field of view.

Tried, and failed. Under the white cotton and navy-blue nylon, the lady was anything but buttoned-down. If anyone appreciated a woman with dangerous curves, it was he. Besides, she'd checked out his package not ten minutes ago, hadn't she? Fair was fair.

The expression in her eyes, when he looked up to meet it a split second too late, had gone from cold to glacial.

"That, Investigator Black, is exactly what I'm talking about. If it turns out you need me to be The Girl—" she infused the words with scorn "—in this investigation, I'll do it on one condition. Respect. Unless, of course, you enjoy defending yourself on harassment charges."

She turned on her heel and left the cube.

Kell pushed himself out of his chair to watch her go, half expecting the office plants to wilt in her wake.

In the bullpen around him, activity had ground to a stop. Even the phones were quiet. The members of the coke team who weren't out chasing Rick O'Reilly stared at him.

He gave them an annoyed glare. "She wants respect, she earns it, just like anybody else around here."

Nobody responded, staring with complete fascination at their computer screens, or shuffling papers from one side of the desk to the other.

Kellan shook his head. "Thanks for the backup. Don't you have a bad guy to chase?"

# 2

LINN PULLED ON A GRAY T-shirt and briefly considered putting a denim jacket over it, then discarded it as too informal. Too approachable. She shrugged into a hip-length black leather coat that went everywhere—even to court, in a pinch—and yanked on plain white socks.

She'd started off on the wrong foot yesterday, despite her success at getting Rick O'Reilly to spill his phone number. Somehow she'd allowed Kellan Black to wriggle past her guard, and he'd unerringly found a way to lodge like a burr, irritating the heck out of her.

No. That wasn't it.

The truth was, Kellan Black wasn't irritating. He was overwhelming. She was a respectable five foot eight, which was two inches taller than the regulation height for female recruits, but he probably stood six-three in bare feet—more, with those motorcycle boots. And it wasn't just that. Every inch of him was packed with sex appeal and testosterone. No wonder she'd retreated into ice-queen mode when he'd smiled at her.

That smile was carnal knowledge and dark secrets and sin. A woman couldn't help but think of climbing over the desk and into the lap of a man who smiled like that, which of course would be a very bad thing if she were looking for the respect of her team.

And he had no business ogling her as if she were a double-scoop sundae and he held a spoon. She squelched the little prickle of pleasure at the memory of the appreciation—no, the downright hunger—in those dark eyes. Thank God she'd worn a practical bra that had hidden the way her nipples had hardened in response. All she needed was to have him know she was attracted to him. He probably had women throwing themselves at him all the time, not to mention a semipermanent one installed at home, as well.

She'd worked hard to get here and wasn't about to jeopardize a career-making opportunity because her team lead looked at her and liked what he saw. She'd spent more months than she cared to think about swimming in the scum-infested waters of California's inner cities, making little marijuana buys and watching her targets go free practically as soon as she charged them. She'd been the only woman in the Santa Rita PD to make her way up the chain of command in the Vetten organization and figure out that Dougie Vetten was bringing his product in to a local marina in pleasure boats. And she'd been the one to arrest him.

Dougie Vetten was the reason she'd been tapped for CLEU, which harvested the best investigators from departments all over the state to take on the criminals everyone thought were untouchable. She was not going to fail now that she'd reached the big time. She was going to work hard, keep her mouth shut and prove to them all that seducing drug dealers into revealing information was a very small part of her working day. No problem.

Right.

At eight o'clock on the dot she walked into the bullpen. Half a dozen surveillance reports still needed to be translated from notes in her notebook to the State's green-and-white forms. She'd been invited to speak to the Silicon Valley Women's Club, so a thirty-minute speech needed to be written and then approved by the Community Relations officer. The tape of yesterday's call had to be sent downstairs for transcription—now there was something for the bug squad's girls to talk about besides the other investigators—and her in box was full of filing that she hadn't gotten around to yet.

With any luck, Kellan and the others had been able to follow Rick O'Reilly yesterday. Get some new names on his associate list. In a perfect world, these would lead them to the person he was getting his product from. And then she'd never have to see him again except when she testified against him in court.

A new poster on the bulletin board caught her eye as she walked toward her cube. In twenty-four-point letters it shouted:

BLACK VS. NICHOLLS
SUDDEN-DEATH SMACKDOWN
TICKETS AVAILABLE IN CUBE W24
GET 'EM WHILE THEY'RE HOT

Cube W24, of course, was Kellan Black's. Linn sighed and debated whether to correct the misspelling of her name in red felt pen and leave the poster there, or to rip it down and tear it to confetti. In the end she merely pulled out the tack that held the poster to the corkboard, folded the paper neatly in thirds and deposited it in the trash.

As she did so, she saw the heads of her teammates doing the gopher thing above their cubes.

"Sorry, boys, the main event's canceled due to lack of interest," she said in a pretty good imitation of a cheerful person, and sat down to work.

When Black himself finally appeared at eighteen minutes to nine, she became very engrossed in the details of Wednesday's surveillance. So engrossed, in fact, that she barely noticed him standing in the door of her space until he spoke.

"He gave us the slip again."

She looked up. "What?"

God, he was big. Big and built and mouthwatering. And all this before he'd probably even had a cup of coffee.

"He disappeared."

Big and built and totally pissed off. "Good morning to you, too. Who did?"

"Tricky Ricky. Try to keep up."

She clenched her molars and bit back the retort he was obviously spoiling for. She understood. He'd lost his target. After all the work they'd done—setting up the call, recording it, locating him—it was disappointing. But there was no need to take it out on her.

"When we got to his location, he was gone. And, of course, the subscriber address on the phone record was a fake."

Without permission, he came in and settled one hip on the corner of her desk. She hoped the modular unit would hold. Then again, it might be fun to see him dumped on his ever-so-sexy butt. He pulled his Get a CLEU cap off and slapped it against his palm. That was no way to treat a cap. If he was going to abuse it, he could give it to her.

"It means I'm back out on the street, hobnobbing with the cream of the underworld society." His tone was even. He was obviously trying hard to put a damper on his temper and be civil. "But we do have a lead."

"I thought you said the address was fake. Did you get something else?"

Slap. "No. You. The Dominion Hotel. Saturday night at nine, remember?"

The breath left her lungs as though an invisible pair of hands had sandwiched her between them and squeezed the air out. She'd forgotten all about her "date." She'd been concentrating more on Kellan Black and his long-lashed brown eyes during that part of her conversation with Ricky, and this was what it got her.

"You're our only hard lead," he went on. "You get to be The Girl again, which I know you're going to enjoy. If you do the meet, we can follow him back to wherever he's hiding now. Open and shut. A couple of hours of work and we're done."

"That was the plan yesterday."

He shook his head and grinned, but she could swear that behind it he was gritting his teeth. "Ah, but now we have the benefit of your skill and experience. I'll brief you so you know everything Dean's girlfriend would be expected to know. Such as my favorite color. What I like you to cook for me. How good I am in bed. Stuff like that."

She kept her face expressionless and refused to respond. "And where will you be while I'm having drinks with him?"

"We'll have to talk that over with the team. Maybe I'll come into the bar and play the jealous boyfriend. O'Reilly already feels he has to compete with me in business. I outsmarted him on some pricing, and he's still pissed about it. Maybe I'll push him some."

So she'd been partly right. That note in O'Reilly's voice hadn't meant that Dean's opinion was important to him; he saw him as a viable competitor, which was good for Dean's rep as a buyer.

"We need to get to his source, and I'm hoping that's the trump card he'll play on me." Kellan got up and crossed to the gap in the fabric walls that constituted a door. "I'll let you know at the briefing."

One hand on the doorjamb, he turned back as if something had just occurred to him. "You've got clothes and stuff, right? He's expecting a hottie, so you'll have to ditch the jeans. He likes bad girls in red, remember?"

He tossed a grin over his shoulder, pulled his cap on and sauntered off down the hall.

A bad girl in red. Something else she'd blanked out while she'd been propositioning Rick O'Reilly and gawking at Kellan Black. Lord only knew what the next obnoxious bulletin-board poster would say once *that* got around.

She wasn't sure she could prepare herself mentally to play a bad girl. A few minutes were one thing. A whole evening convincing some scumball that she wanted to go to bed with him was quite another. That, and dealing with Jealous Guy, who she would bet her next paycheck would play it to the hilt. The whole meet could blow up in her face, and take her career with it.

Although, she admitted deep in that dark place inside that gave her a jolt of sexual energy every time Kellan Black smiled, driving a man like him to jealousy—even if it were pretend—might be fun.

The cover team wanted the main event, did they? Thought they had her all figured out?

*Come on, boys. It's show time.*

"'HE LIKES BAD GIRLS IN RED'? Why don't you just wave a red flag in front of the EEOC?" Cooper Maxwell stretched his legs under Kellan's desk and folded his arms. "Not paying attention again in diversity class, were we?"

Kellan hadn't meant to badger the woman, but damn, he was up against it. "Get out of my chair." Cooper obligingly moved to the guest chair. Kellan dropped into his own and leaned his elbows on the paper on his desk. "What am I going to do? I can waste another week hanging out in seedy bars and chasing cockroaches through apartment buildings, looking for O'Reilly, or I can use my one brilliant lead and go straight to him."

The only problem was the brilliant lead. She was a member of his team in name only. He hadn't chosen her the way he'd handpicked the rest of his guys—she'd been assigned to him because she was female and because CLEU had to comply with the Equal Employment Opportunity Commission's regulations, just like any other State entity.

"She seems kinda reluctant to get into the spirit of the thing. Go with the flow. Enjoy the thrill of the chase and all that," Cooper mused. "Then again, maybe she just has a healthy respect for her own life. I can remember a few times when the thrill of the chase had me staring down the barrel of an automatic."

In his saner moments Kellan might be able to empathize. He'd messed up the odd investigation and earned the censure of everybody on the unit. But at least he was willing to get out there and do what he could to beat back the tide of drugs rolling onto the shores of the continent, thanks to lowlifes like Rick O'Reilly.

"I don't care." His tone was blunt. "I have a job to do, and by God, I'm going to do it, even if it means partnering an EEOC princess with a split personality."

Coop grinned. "And some personality it is, too. If you come in tomorrow with your rocks frozen off, don't say I didn't warn you."

His buddy sauntered back to his desk, leaving Kellan to stare sightlessly at the mess on his own. Linn Nichols wasn't the kind of woman he cared to spend time with, but he'd be curious to know what it took to make personality number two come out to play. Kellan kicked back in his chair and propped his boots on the desk. Did the luscious Caroline show herself on weekends, or only under pressure, when Linn was backed into a corner and had to get creative?

And most intriguing of all, was she made up, just an act, or a part of Linn's inner self, kept carefully locked up under "I'm not a woman, I'm a drone" clothes?

Kellan shook his head and pulled his keyboard onto his knee. He had to stop thinking about his co-worker's personal life and habits. Fraternizing with someone on your own team was a bad idea. It got too uncomfortable when relationships fizzled and you still had to see the person every day. It was a lot safer to have a quick fling with the out-of-town operators. Everybody knew the ropes. A couple of nights of fun, then drive her to the airport, no hard feelings.

He started to type. "File 04-0117. 7/18, 10:00 hours." He paused, then minimized the report and brought up the "compose" screen on his e-mail instead.

To: lnichols@cleu.ca.gov
From: kblack@cleu.ca.gov
Re: shopping
I'm betting Caroline doesn't have anything appropriate to wear Saturday night. We've got to do this right. Pick you up tonight after work.
Kell

# 3

LINN STARED AT HER E-MAIL. He bet she didn't have anything sexy to wear, did he?

She did so. She had a black-velvet cocktail dress that she'd not only worn on bodyguard duty at an embassy do here in San Francisco, but that she'd actually taken on a cruise once.

It wasn't red, though. And it sounded as though CLEU was catering to Rick O'Reilly's horrible taste in women's clothing for purposes of this investigation. Well, she didn't have to cater to it. Caroline wouldn't wear something just because some guy told her to. Caroline had a bit of spine.

Linn would just make good and sure she was out of here when swing shift came in, and she'd take off and do something else instead of going home. Look as he might, Kellan Black wouldn't be able to track her down.

Because of course he'd try. Her profile was in the CLEU database, and a few keystrokes would tell him everything he wanted to know, including her address, how old she was, and how many years she'd spent in school. *Confidential* meant nothing to these guys. Breaking into the Human Resources computer files was finger practice, as commonplace as getting a cup of coffee. Easier. They didn't even have to get up.

In the underground parking lot, she scanned the unmarked vehicles that sat in a row separate from the investigators' personal cars and trucks. Since CLEU was not a police department, they didn't own marked cars, but the undercover cars were still equipped with hidden sirens and lights. The sporty, high-performance two-door that had appeared when Kellan did yesterday was gone.

Linn unlocked her vehicle and got in. Shopping, indeed. Ha. He'd have to find her first.

She made it to the first intersection past CLEU headquarters when he did.

Directly behind her, a police siren blurted on, then off. When she ignored it, she heard it again, sustained long enough to get her attention. Linn glanced in the rearview mirror and saw him in the sports car the California taxpayers had provided him, large as life, grinning as he flipped the siren on and off like a rapper with a turntable. The flashing lights concealed in the grille blinked in time with the noise.

Damn! She checked traffic on all sides, but there was no way to lose him, unless she wanted instant death by attempting a high-speed chase in the middle of the financial district. She drove into the parking lot of an espresso bar. By the time he pulled in beside her, she was leaning on the rear fender of her little hatchback SUV, arms crossed, waiting impatiently, as if she had something much more important to do and he was holding her up.

His physicality was just as potent in the open air as it was in the office. She rested the backs of her knees against the bumper of her vehicle to ground herself with something solid.

"Knocking off early?" he asked with an easy smile, settling against the back of his own car as if he had all the time in the world. "Going home to change?"

"No," she said. "I had plans this evening."

"Not a problem. Reschedule 'em."

"I will not."

"Come on, Linn. You're my only hope. My only lead to O'Reilly. I told you, we have to do this right, and that means the right look and the right information."

"I'm perfectly capable of coming up with the right look. I've done this before, you know."

"Yeah, I know. So what do you call the right look? Black velvet and pearls?"

She felt a little nettled. "That's what I had in mind, yes."

"Linn, this is California, not Boston."

"I know this is California. This is where I've had all my training. Your problem is, you don't want me taking control, even with something as inconsequential as what I wear."

He gave her a narrow look. "I'm the case lead. You have a problem with me wanting control?"

Uh-oh. He may look like every woman's dream

of a night of sin, but he had the same hierarchical mindset of every cop she'd ever known. The last thing she wanted was the ugly word *insubordination* in her performance evaluation.

"Of course not." She bit off the words with difficulty.

"Then get over it. We're going to get you a dress, and since the meet is day after tomorrow, we're going now. Get on the horn and cancel your plans."

With an effort she didn't care if he saw, she controlled her temper and spoke in a tone that was almost calm. "It's all right. They weren't firmed up anyway."

He accepted her words at face value. Evidently he was the kind of man who let bygones be bygones— once he'd gotten his own way.

"Great. Leave your car at the office where it's more secure and we'll take Victor-21."

She doubted anybody would want to steal a five-year-old vehicle that didn't even have power windows, but she did as he suggested.

When she slid into the passenger seat of his car— call code Victor-21—he waited politely for her to buckle in before he gunned it up the ramp and out onto the street.

She had never understood people with claustrophobia before, but now she got an inkling of what it was like to be trapped in a small space without enough air. She rolled the window down an inch, enough to let in the breeze off San Francisco Bay, flavored generously with exhaust fumes and the smell of frying fish.

The guy took up way too much room. Or maybe it wasn't just him. There was something in the air between them. Sexual awareness on her side. Oh, yeah. And what else? Challenge? Was this little excursion some kind of a test?

If so, she was going to pass it. No problem. How hard could it be to find a dress that only a bad girl would wear?

"So." He piloted the car as if it were a fighter jet. "What kind of clothes does Caroline like?"

"I have no idea," Linn retorted a little acidly. "She didn't exist before yesterday."

"Oh, I bet she did." He gave her a sideways glance that hinted at drizzled chocolate and French kisses and things better left unmentioned in the daytime.

She gave herself a shake. This had to stop. The guy had "catch the crook" on his mind, nothing more. She was projecting flirtation onto him because…well, because it was a better alternative than what she'd been thinking since yesterday, which was jumping on him.

He leaned over to look into her face. "You okay?"

*Stop it, Nichols.* She had no business dwelling so much on someone she'd known for two days. "Yes. I was just thinking."

"About what?"

"About clothes."

"Is that all?"

"Yes, that's all," she lied. "I'll need something I can run in if I have to, which narrows down the field."

"You won't need to run. The cover team and I will be there."

"You do your job, I'll do mine. And if it makes me more comfortable to operate in clothes I can run in, I'll do it."

"You can run in a miniskirt, right?"

She gave up. He was not going to let her do this her way. "Yes," she sighed.

Fortunately for her patience and his immediate survival, they arrived at the mall. Within minutes she'd found a boutique that carried clothes that might be appropriate for picking up drug dealers, although the management probably wouldn't thank her for saying so.

"What's your size?" Kellan studied a rack of dresses with an appraising eye.

"Look, Kellan, I can find a red dress. How hard can it be?" Two salesgirls who looked about seventeen were descending on them. She had to get him out of here before he said something truly embarrassing. "Why don't you go to the electronics store or something?"

He glanced at her, one brow raised incredulously. "What for? I have a job to do here. For this op, you need to look classy, even if the next stop after the bar is the bedroom. So to speak."

She stared at him. "Bar. Bedroom. Class. Mutually exclusive."

"Nah. Not for Caroline. She can pull it off."

Naturally both salesgirls arrived in time to hear him. "A classy woman who can be convinced otherwise," one of them said, and gave Linn an all-over inspection. "Sleek. Feminine. A woman with secrets. Is this for you or someone else?"

Linn did not want to explain why her companion was referring to her in the third person. "For me."

"I want to see you in them." Kellan pulled up a chair outside the dressing room and straddled it backward. "No hiding in the changeroom the way my sisters do, and saying everything makes you look fat."

Linn clamped her teeth together for the second time that day. If this kept up she was going to start sending him her dental bills.

And the man had sisters. Funny, she'd been thinking of him as a solo act, isolated by the nature of his job. It seemed strange to think of him as someone with a family. Sisters were something they had in common, but his probably didn't sneak into his room and borrow his clothes.

Then again, maybe they did. She had a concert T-shirt somewhere in her T-shirt drawer herself. It was for Stevie Ray Vaughan, though, not Aerosmith.

Linn hung up the dresses in the change room and got down to business. The first dress was about forty percent leather. The other sixty percent was…missing. She didn't have to wear a bra with it, but the air-conditioning seeped under the leather in places air-conditioning didn't usually go.

"No on this one," she informed him through the dressing room door.

"Why not?" She heard the chair legs scrape the floor as he got up.

"Don't you dare!" She flung the door open and glared at him, and his critical gaze slid from shoulders to hem.

Thank God for the leather. It hid her nipples, which were hardening under his perusal, and there was no way on earth she wanted him to know that.

"No," he said at last. "You want to seduce the guy, not tie him up and beat him."

Linn shut the door in his face and pulled off the leather.

The next one seemed more like a slip, something she would wear *under* her black velvet. She felt undressed, incomplete. Cold. The bra may not be the best fashion choice, but under this dress, it was vital.

When she stepped out of the dressing room, Kellan's eyes lit up. "That's it."

"Ditch the bra," the salesgirl said.

"No. Ditch the dress." She shut the dressing room door again, a little more firmly than necessary.

"Come on, Linn," Kellan said through the door. "It's perfect for Caroline."

The salesgirl could make what she wanted of that one, Linn thought. "It's burgundy. Not red." She yanked the satiny thing over her head. "Besides, I'm the one who has to wear it, so I get veto power."

Even without a bra, she could appear in public in the third one—made of some filmy fabric that resembled silk crepe—without getting arrested by her own cover team. She looked over her shoulder at the back, reflected in the dressing room mirror.

Or maybe not.

It *had* no back. The front was decent enough—a boat neck that bared her collarbone. No sleeves. But the back plunged to the waist and left more skin visible than she had ever displayed outside her bedroom. Not only that, the flared skirt was short. Really short. Some serious engineering was going to have to occur in the underwear department to make this one work.

She stepped out of the dressing room.

Kellan's gaze traveled over her slowly, taking in every stitch, lingering on the way the crepe fabric draped over her breasts, which were obviously naked underneath. This time his gaze wasn't critical. Far from it. The look in his eyes made her skin heat up. Her nipples tightened, and the material formed a crescent-shaped swag from one to the other where it had merely draped a moment ago.

His eyes met hers, and she felt a jolt of desire in the pit of her belly. Between one second and the next, she realized, he had gone from seeing her as an operative who needed to be outfitted, to a woman, a sexual being, who was displaying herself for him. If he could have this kind of effect just by looking at her, what would happen if he kissed her? Or, God, made love to her?

"Better." He sounded as if he'd just remembered he ought to say something.

"Do you like it?" the salesgirl chirped, and broke the spell. Cinderella came back to earth in the dressing room with a jolt.

"This is definitely a woman who can be convinced," the girl went on. "We can get you a no-strap bra to go under that, if you want."

*Now you tell me,* Linn thought, trying to recover. She turned and let him get an eyeful of the back, keeping her face out of his line of sight.

It was Caroline who enjoyed a man looking at her. Caroline who bought red dresses. Not she, Linn. By the time this case was over, she was going to have to check herself into the loony bin with acute schizophrenia.

"Good choice." Kellan's voice still sounded a little strange, as if he were having a hard time getting out the words. He cleared his throat. "Okay, Linn?"

The department was going to pay for it, she knew that much. Caroline might buy clothes like this, but in Linn's book, if you couldn't wear something to work, you shouldn't waste the budget on it.

*But you are wearing this to work.* Well, yes, she thought, in a manner of speaking.

*And Kellan likes it.* Kellan probably liked hockey and beer, too, but she wasn't about to go buy a sixty-inch television and a case of Coors now, was she?

*You like it that Kellan likes it.*

That was going to have to stop, ASAP.

Silencing the voice from the dark side, Linn turned back into the dressing room. She slid into her comfortable clothes with a sense of relief. The jacket was her choice. She looked like herself in it—clean and classic.

Not like a woman who could be convinced.

Not like Caroline.

KELLAN FLICKED A GLANCE at Linn while he waited for the light to change. She held the shopping bag on her lap as if it contained something that should be disposed of by the HazMat team.

The problem with her was that she was too structured. Too controlled. No imagination. Trying on a red dress was probably the most excitement she'd had since senior prom.

Or so he tried to tell himself. He was still in recovery from that moment in the dressing room when he'd realized just how desirable and touchable this woman could be. And now he was having a hard time getting his view of her back to where it had been.

Where it was safe.

Some people, he knew, liked an eight-to-five gig where things stayed the same from day to day, where you knew exactly what you'd walk in and do every morning. A person like that belonged in Motor Vehicles, not CLEU. He loved coming in and not knowing what was going to happen. When they'd pulled him out of the Sacramento PD to join this specialized State unit, he couldn't have been happier. Not that he was an adrenaline junkie. He wasn't like his predecessor, who had faked his way through the psych screens so well that no one had figured out that the higher than normal numbers of casualties on his cases were the result of him going off like a cannon in life-and-death situations, just for the high.

No, Kellan wasn't a fool with life—his or anybody else's—but he was okay with a little risk if it meant getting the collar. And the woman next to him was definitely a risk. An unknown.

One with a beautifully honed body that could bring a man begging to his knees. The memory of the way that red silk had clung was going to keep him up at night for a long time.

"Do you have anything going on tomorrow night?" he asked.

Only a flicker of her eyelids told him he'd startled her by breaking the silence. "What do you mean?"

"I mean do you have plans. We need to get together again so I can brief you."

She glanced at him, then straight ahead. "The light is green."

So it was. He stepped on the accelerator.

"Why can't you brief me during office hours? Or right now?"

He heard a tiny *pop* as one of her nails punctured the plastic bag, and frowned. "I'm in court tomorrow and I have to prep for that tonight. The O'Reilly case will take time to go through with you. It's a lot of material. Fills a whole box. I even have an org chart to show you where I fit into his command structure."

She sighed and chewed the inside of her cheek. She looked indecisive. Vulnerable. His determination to see her strictly as a means to an investigative end careered off the track again.

Well, hell. Why the hesitation? If he had anything but this single card to play, he would. An evening with him wasn't that bad, was it? Maybe he'd better throw something in to sweeten the pot.

"I'll take you to dinner. We can discuss it over Dungeness at the Crab Factory, if you want."

"Wouldn't we be overheard?"

"It's possible. But not likely."

"You can't take file folders and org charts to the Crab Factory."

She was right. "Okay then, how about I take them to your place? We can eat and do the briefing there, and not have to worry about people listening in." When the silence got a little too long, he glanced over. "What?"

"I…I'm not sure."

"I don't care if you're a lousy housekeeper."

She straightened, and her lips thinned. "There's nothing wrong with my domestic skills."

"Then what's the problem?"

"We could just use a conference room at the office. Or go to your place."

The lady didn't want him in her house. She probably didn't want him to see that she had prissy little plastic slipcovers on all the furniture, like his grandma. If he didn't care about where the briefing would be before, he definitely cared now.

He wanted to see where she lived.

"We could, I suppose," he mused. "I just got this really great king-size bed. It's so big I almost couldn't get the TV into—"

"Fine," she snapped. "Come to my place. You won't get Dungeness, but I'll think of something."

She dictated the address, but he'd already had Coop break into her HR profile. He'd memorized it the way he memorized license plates and the telephone numbers of his suspects.

"What time?" He spun the wheel and dove down the ramp into the CLEU parking lot, rolling to a stop next to her little Japanese knockoff.

"Will you be out of court by six?" Her tone was civil in the extreme. She was trying to get them back on a business footing, too. That was good, right?

"Yes."

"See you then." She closed the passenger door and climbed into her car without another glance at him, tossing the shopping bag onto the seat beside her as if it hadn't just cost the State the price of a bribe.

He watched her pull away while Victor-21's engine idled. Then he parked the unmarked car in its assigned space and got into his own truck. While he waited for it to warm up, he tried to figure out Linn Nichols.

How could a woman so dislike the clothes that made her look that good? Legs like hers under a dress like that were enough to get her arrested. But at work, half a dozen identical sets of blue jeans did a fine job of hiding them from curious eyes.

He'd seen her body respond when she knew he was looking at her. Was Caroline lurking behind those eyes somewhere?

No. Couldn't be.

But the possibility intrigued him a lot more than it should.

Abruptly he decided to play the jealous boyfriend Saturday night. He might only get one chance to get cozy with Caroline, and damned if he was going to let Tricky Ricky have all the fun.

# 4

THE WAY LINN SAW IT, she had two choices. She could accept the damned assignment and play The Girl to the hilt, or she could resist and demand to be given meaningful duties that resulted in the respect she craved.

The problem was, she was a Libra, and Libras saw things from both sides. On the other side of the scale, Kellan Black really did have only one option, and that was to use her as Caroline. He'd run every other lead into the ground, and was banking his success on her. What she couldn't know was whether playing Caroline would work. If it did, and the operation succeeded, she had a fighting chance at being accepted by the team.

But the cost...could she pay the price?

She wished she could talk through this with someone. She could call Natalie Wong at the Santa Rita PD, but the chances of having an uninterrupted conversation while Nat was at work were pretty much nil. She could call her sister, Tessa, but she was probably still in class. Besides, talking about work with her family was like trying to communicate through a door—you got some things through, but rarely the important ones. Her parents and Tessa happily marched to their own drums, whereas Linn had deliberately chosen to march to one that was tried and true, and came with a retirement plan.

Like law enforcement. You always knew where you were with the law. She just wished she could say the same about her team. Or her team lead.

She'd sleepwalked through paperwork and a surveillance today while he'd been in court. A glance at the clock told her she didn't have time to spend on the phone, anyway. She had an hour to shower, change and get dinner started before he was due to arrive.

In the shower she reached for her handmade aromatherapy soap, scented with lime and some herb that always made her feel alert and positive. No plain-Jane brand-name soap for her, no sir. She knew she was a white-cotton, tailored kind of woman. A strong, no-nonsense woman who took things on and got them done. But that didn't mean she couldn't have a few tiny vices. Handmade soap and a glass of Baileys straight up in the evening did something toward balancing the stress and frustration of the job.

It was a better alternative than pharmaceuticals, at any rate. Cheaper, too.

The soap foamed over her skin and washed away the interminable day, leaving her feeling at least a little optimistic that she could get through a meeting with Kellan Black without killing him or crawling into his lap—both of which she wanted badly and which would be very dangerous for her career.

Linn stood naked in front of her closet and fingered the skirt of the red silk dress hanging on the back of the door. She could just imagine the cover team's reaction when she walked into the hotel bar in this. Just like Kellan in the dressing room, they'd never look at her in the same way again. They'd think of her as a sexual object, not as a fellow investigator, and she couldn't stand the thought of it. She'd paid her dues on that score with the Santa Rita PD.

But for some reason she couldn't figure out, with Kellan it was different. Face it, she liked that look in his eyes. Wanted to see it again, in fact. And since she was never going to get to see it in real life because he was her team lead, and any kind of looking along that line was strictly against State human resources policies, the only way she was going to satisfy her craving was to play Caroline.

Which, she was sure, was sick and twisted and likely to get her sent up to the staff therapist when it was all over.

So what would happen if she played Caroline tonight?

He'd said himself that she needed to know everything Dean's girlfriend would be likely to know. What better way to do that than to reach down into that dark place inside her and bring Caroline out, just for this briefing? Caroline was the kind of woman who got the upper hand through sex, not through hard work. Men fell all over themselves to invite her to their lovely houses—and paid for the privilege.

Kellan Black would look at Caroline and she'd revel in it, to hell with the HR rules.

Besides, it wasn't as if she were going to sleep with him. It was only dinner. And practice at being his girlfriend. Totally job related.

Highly unethical. But job related.

The red dress was out of the question, of course. She might get a spot on it and there wouldn't be time to get it to the cleaners before tomorrow night. Among all these clothes she must have something that Caroline would wear to a cozy dinner at home with her boyfriend Dean.

Of course, Caroline would probably wear nothing at all. Maybe she'd cook him his pasta in a black satin thong. But there were limits to how far Linn was prepared to go in the interests of prepping for her part.

Linn dug through the slacks, skirts and shirts she owned, without success. Then, way at the back, her hand fell on a black leather miniskirt that her little sister had talked her into a couple of years ago. Tessa had taken up the weird hobby of reading tarot and styling herself as a psychic, and somehow the black leather skirt had played into Linn's future. Linn blanked on exactly how, but in a moment of madness she'd bought the skirt, just to keep Tessa quiet.

Tess had been wrong about Linn's future—the skirt couldn't do much about it, tucked away in the dark—but maybe it could influence Caroline's.

And Kellan's. Ha.

Okay, what went with a black leather skirt? She

had a pile of T-shirts and tank tops, but most were what she wore to the gym. A cotton camisole was a possibility, but it had seen better days. Caroline would never put on something that had gone yellow around the edges.

She eyed a white tailored shirt. Hmm. *A black lace bra,* whispered Kensington W8. *The shirt over it, with the top half-dozen buttons undone. I'd wear that.*

Great. Now she was hearing voices.

*I'm part of you, darling. You can do this. Why, you could have that man for dessert if you wanted to.*

Linn rolled her eyes. And wouldn't she have some explaining to do to Lieutenant Bryan?

This was risky, she thought as she shimmied into the skirt and bra, and hesitated on the buttons of the shirt. She hoped Kellan Black was the strong, silent type, because if he did what most investigators did, which was run their mouths off about their sex lives at every possible opportunity, she might as well kiss her career at CLEU goodbye.

*Undo one more button.*

Fine. Linn put her hands on her hips, which made the placket of the shirt spread, and bent forward.

It was clear she was going to get her money's worth out of her lingerie tonight.

*Lovely, darling. Now makeup.*

Oops. She'd almost forgotten makeup. Obviously a swipe of lip gloss and a couple of strokes of mascara weren't going to cut it with Caroline.

When she was finished, Linn gave herself a critical look in the bathroom mirror. Her eyes were sultry and long-lashed, her lips full and red. She looked like someone who could not only take on Kellan Black or Rick O'Reilly, but…what was it Kellan had said? Oh, yes. Tie him up and beat him, too.

The thought made her smile, and on the heels of it, the bell rang.

*Show time, darling.*

KELLAN STOOD OUTSIDE the town house door and looked around him curiously. Nice place. Nicer than his, but that wouldn't take much. Linn's complex in the upscale town of San Mateo was designed around a series of courtyards, with trees and flowers and a fake stream that probably cost the homeowners' association a bundle in maintenance. But the shade felt good in the heat of the July evening.

Beside the steps, someone had planted a bed of blood-red peonies. His mom's favorite. She was retired now, but when she'd had the florist shop in Modesto, he could remember helping her and seeing her bury her face in a big bouquet of them. Not to smell them, she'd said. To feel the petals against her skin.

That was his mom. Hugging everyone—kids, peonies, dogs, you name it. And teaching him and his two older sisters the names of all the flowers in both Latin and English. He still remembered a lot of them.

He'd forgotten how to hug, though.

A lot of cops let the paranoia of knowing how bad the bad guys were get to them. And the time on the street just exacerbated it. The time you poured into the job messed up marriages, destroyed families, left good cops washed up on the shores of permanent therapy. He'd started relationships with the best of intentions and then somewhere along the road he'd given more of himself to the job than to the person he was supposed to be with, and potential life partners had fallen along the wayside.

That was why he gravitated to women who knew the price of the job as well as he did. Women in law enforcement who weren't looking for long-term. Who knew how to have fun and didn't bother with consequences.

Women like, well, the imaginary Caroline.

The bottle of wine he held chilled his fingers, and when a trickle of sweat snaked down his back under his shirt, he considered holding it against the back of his neck. Probably not the best thing to do to a decent wine before he offered it to his hostess, though.

The door opened, and he stepped back in surprise, catching himself on the wrought-iron railing just before he took a header off her low front step and crushed the peonies.

"Linn?" Maybe he was hallucinating Caroline. Or maybe Linn had a gorgeous twin sister, come for a visit.

"Don't you recognize me, darling? Here, give me that wine before you drop it."

No hallucination. Buttoned-up Linn Nichols was definitely unbuttoned now, and playing the evening as Caroline. Somebody up there loved him. He should run out and buy a lottery ticket, but then he'd lose half an hour of the evening with her, and he wasn't going to let that happen.

She leaned in and he sucked in a breath as her breasts snugged against his chest, heavy and sweet. The teasing scent of lime wafted past him in the second before her mouth touched his lightly, and then she was gone. His stunned brain hadn't even had time to command his arms to move around her.

"Guh," he said, and gave himself a mental slap. He followed her into the kitchen and tried again. "How…how are you?"

"I'm very well, thanks." She smiled at him over her shoulder as she stirred something in a pan, and he felt his brain cells sizzle. That smile was dazzling, and combined with those eyes and that—he blinked—skirt. Leather skirt. Bare legs. Bare feet, slipped into glossy little flip-flops with a black flower between her toes.

Maybe he'd better buy two tickets.

"Is everything all right?" she asked.

"Oh, yeah."

"I meant with your case this afternoon."

He stared at her blankly, and his brain cleared. "It was fine. Going to trial. Man, you have the best… uh…English accent I've ever heard."

"I spent a term at Oxford during college. It's difficult not to pick it up. I thought it would be appropriate for this evening."

*Appropriate* had never sounded so inappropriate as her upper-class accent contrasted with those luscious lips pouting into a kiss with every *p*. He wondered if he could get her to say *popcorn*. Or *pornographic*.

Or *suspended*, the last remaining rational part of his brain reminded him. *This is Linn, you dummy. Your teammate. Your off-limits teammate who threatened you with a lawsuit the day you met her.*

So why were his responses escalating every time he saw her? Was it because every time he saw her, she was another step deeper into her role as Caroline?

They were the same woman.

Maybe it was he who had the problem. A woman like Caroline had "short-term" written all over her, and a woman like Linn meant "unwrap carefully—serious investment inside." Maybe his body already knew what his mind refused: this woman presented a challenge he wasn't going to be able to resist.

Scary thought. One he wasn't ready for.

She was looking at him expectantly. He thought back quickly to what she'd just said and got his mind back on track. Accent. Job. That was it.

"So you're playing Caroline tonight for a little practice?"

"Yes. Do you like it?"

"Well, it'll get me in the mood before tomorrow," he said. No doubt about that. "It'll remind me we're supposed to be sleeping together, not working together."

"Oh, I'll make sure you remember."

That smile again, seductive, over her shoulder. Kellan wondered how he was going to survive the evening without dragging her into the bedroom and tearing off her clothes. If she were only wearing something sensible under her white shirt, he could maybe keep his mind on business. But she wasn't. The fabric half revealed something black and lacy and definitely not sensible. It was meant to be looked at, and right now, he wanted to do that more than anything he could remember wanting to do in a long time.

She drained the pasta and tossed it with a mixture from another pan that looked like scallops, clams and crisp, colorful vegetables. "Not very fancy, I'm afraid. I hope you're not allergic to shellfish."

It looked pretty fancy to him. He couldn't remember the last time he'd actually cooked in his apartment. If he didn't grab something in the CLEU cafeteria, he usually stopped for a hamburger or went out with Coop.

"I'm not allergic to anything. It looks great."

"You could open the wine."

He found her corkscrew and got to work as close to her as possible. In the galley kitchen, it wasn't that hard.

"How long can you sustain the accent?"

"The longer I do it, the easier it is. I could go months."

"It won't take that long to catch O'Reilly. Besides, I'm about done with the whole organization. Another couple of weeks is all I can stand."

The cork popped out, and she took the bottle from him. Her hand slid lovingly down its neck and his brain shorted out again. In a trance, he watched her pour.

"You keep promising me you'll catch him, but evidently you're a man who likes to take his time."

His hand jerked as he took a glass from her, and a little wine splashed on the counter. "Sorry." He grabbed the dishcloth from the sink and mopped up the little spill. He had to get a grip. If he went to pieces every time she said things like this tomorrow night, he was going to look like a basket case, and worse, O'Reilly would know they weren't sleeping together.

Besides, Kellan was used to being the one in charge. The pursuer. The one with all the great lines. It was time to see that Caroline got as good as she was giving.

Linn, he reminded himself.

Whoever.

She waved him into a seat at a round, antique-looking dining table that could seat four if she tried hard. Either she didn't have many dinner parties for more than two, or she had huge ones and fed them all buffet style out on the neatly trimmed lawn he could see through the sliding glass door.

His gaze followed the riot of feathery purple flowers that made up the border between the lawn and a couple of pine trees.

"Did you plant the salvia?" he asked.

She glanced over her shoulder to see what he was looking at. "The what?"

"The Mexican sage. The purple ones where those hummingbirds are. See them?"

"Oh, those. Yes, I did. What did you call it?"

"*Salvia leucantha*. My mom was a florist before she retired. I have a good memory for names and numbers, including stuff most people don't care about, like the Latin names of plants."

"Is she still alive?"

"Oh, yeah. Everybody's in Sacramento."

"You have sisters, too, right?"

"How did you know?"

She offered the pasta to him, and opened a small china container containing freshly shredded Parmesan cheese.

"Thanks." He liked his pasta bristly with cheese. The real stuff, not the shredded plastic that came in a cardboard tube. He spooned it out with a generous hand.

"You mentioned it when we were getting the dress last night."

He had? He took a healthy sip of his wine. "Where's your family?"

"I'm not sure."

What did that mean? Had they all run away?

"My sister's up in the City doing graduate work at U.C.S.F., so I know where she is. My parents left in a motorhome a couple of years ago and in the last postcard they said they were in Santa Fe."

He nodded. "Retired?"

"I don't know what from, but they say so. My mom's a painter and my dad plays at being a writer." She gestured into the living room, and he wondered how he could have missed the huge painting that hung over the couch.

"Your mom did that?" It was amazing, and his knowledge of art would fit in a salt shaker. Bold curves arced over the canvas in brilliant shades from apple green to blue to fiery yellow. "What is it?"

"It's called *Sunbather.*"

He squinted. "A woman lying on a hill? Or in a garden?"

"Everyone sees something different. I thought it was a beach."

Maybe it was a beach. "Maybe that violet-blue part is water."

"Or maybe it's a garden and that's the salvia."

He turned back to look at her and fell into her smile—the first warm, real smile he'd ever seen. A moment ago he'd wanted to find out about her family, about the mother who used color in as sensual a way as his own mother used flowers.

But now he was caught in her smile, in a vibration of awareness that flickered between them, drawing them together whether they wanted to be or not.

Kellan broke the contact, dug into his pasta and tried for a fast recovery. He came up blank.

Linn shifted in her chair, and when she spoke, the English accent was back. "I thought you were bringing in your file folders and organization charts."

"They're all in the truck. I'll get them after we eat."

"Tell me how you got to O'Reilly." They were back to business with a vengeance. "I'd be interested to know how you got past all the levels in his organization."

He laid down his fork. "You know, it's really disconcerting to hear you talk business in that accent. I don't know whether I'm talking to Caroline or to Linn."

"Which would you prefer, darling?" she asked, in exactly the same tone she'd used on Tricky Ricky the other day. Just before she'd offered him a blow job.

"Talking to Caroline keeps me in character, but I need to talk to Linn."

"You needn't think of me as two people, you know. I'm not Sybil."

"Oh, yes, you are." He speared a broccoli floret with his fork and pointed it at her. "Caroline is as far from Linn as—as I am from Rick O'Reilly."

"What's he like?" She sipped her wine and he watched her lips touch the glass and part.

"Who?"

"Rick O'Reilly. Do keep up."

He concentrated on his food and not her mouth. He wasn't going to think about how he could surprise her into smiling again. "He knows how to work people. He has a nose for their weaknesses and goes right for them. Naturally he rose in the ranks."

"So has he found your weakness?"

"Not yet. That's why he went for you. He thinks he can use you to get to me."

"He's very quick. We hadn't talked for more than a few minutes."

"See what I mean?"

"If you're going to set him up for a deal, how do I fit in?"

"We let him think his plan is working. The only reason he's been so successful so far is that he always lets the other guy take the fall. There's no honor among thieves here. If he gets backed into a corner, he'll throw someone into the line of fire to save himself. If he thinks you're my weakness he'll try to set things up so that he winds up in the Caymans with you and the product, and Dean winds up in the slammer."

"Won't he be surprised."

"Yeah. Little does he know we could have taken him down after the two-kilo buy we did a few days ago, and made it stick."

"What happened?"

"I'd been working up to it for months. You know, a half pound of product here from one of his people, a pound there. I did a smaller one with O'Reilly himself at the beginning of the month, and that primed him to trust me for the two keys. So the State had to ante up for that. I wanted to take him down and get the money back before he spent it all."

"But then you wouldn't get the guy above him. Do you have any ideas as to who that is?"

"All we know from various hints O'Reilly has dropped is that he's Colombian. I'd like to get his in-country lab and their suppliers, too, but my expectations are reasonable. My goal is to get O'Reilly to introduce me. That's the other part of your job. You're a jet-setter. You're giving me some international flavor, especially with Hidalgo to vouch for you."

Kellan cleaned the last of the pasta off his plate and was surprised to find there was no more left in the bowl. "That was really good. Did I eat all that?"

"I like a man with healthy appetites."

He calmed the jolt in his blood and pointed his fork at her a second time. "Stop that."

"I'm in character, darling."

"You're too damn good. I keep forgetting I'm your team lead."

Her smile was slow and lovely, full of pleasure at the confession. "I thought that was the point."

She had him there. The problem was, by rights he should only respond to her when he was working, as Dean. But Kellan didn't want to settle for that.

He wanted her himself.

# 5

LINN WAS WILLING TO BET that Kellan Black hadn't been this off balance since, oh, maybe kindergarten. And even then he was probably batting his brown eyes at the little girls and bewitching them into giving him their cookies at snack time.

But she held all the cookies now.

He shouldered the front door open, and she closed it behind him while he settled a file box and a huge, accordion-pleated folder on her coffee table. It would have been too much to hope that his files would be like hers—in date order and organized with tabs and indexes. Oh, no. It looked as if an explosion had happened deep inside the file, and sure enough, the moment he set it down, it tipped over and spilled its contents all over her hardwood floor.

"Aw, crap."

"Here, I'll get them."

"No, I know where everything is."

That was hard to believe.

"We might as well start with this stuff." He scooped up a folder that looked exactly like every other folder in the mess. "Here's that org chart."

The document was filled with labeled boxes branching off a central tree. Lots of labeled boxes. Here was where he got orderly, it seemed.

"Color coding. Very nice."

"I had to figure out some way of keeping everybody straight. The empty box in the top row is our eventual target, the Colombian. All I know after six months in this organization is that he owns property in California and possibly other states. For the last month I've been working on getting his name. This two-kilo deal we just did with O'Reilly was supposed to grease the way to an introduction and The Big One, but so far Rick isn't giving me so much as the guy's initials."

"What's it like, being in deep cover for so long?"

Silence stretched out for a moment while he gazed at the chart.

"It's dangerous," he said at last. "There are days when I'm terrified and all I want to do is come out. Then there are days when I'm so into it I don't ever want to come out." He paused, then said so softly that she wasn't sure he remembered she was there, "Those days scare me even worse."

After a moment he seemed to collect himself and pointed to the chart. When he spoke, his voice was completely normal, as though she hadn't interrupted at all.

"Rick and I are on the next level down, in red boxes. The distributors below us are blue. On my side, of course, they're mostly imaginary, but I've had Coop and Danny make themselves visible when they're needed. When we do the roundup, teams will arrest these guys as well as O'Reilly. Below them, the street-level traffickers are green. They'll probably disappear into the woodwork like rats, and we probably won't waste too many resources on them. Last, our informants are orange. They're scattered on every level."

In the row of blue distributors, the box for Hidalgo Martinez, the confidential informant they'd managed to flip, was orange, as were several among the street-level dealers.

"This is great," she murmured. "I'll need to memorize it."

He handed her a fat manila folder. "This is the file on Rick, as well as the few facts I have about the Colombian. You can keep it tonight to learn as much about them as you can before the meet. I'll need it back in the morning."

In the five minutes it had taken him to go out to the car and get the files, he'd evidently managed to forget that brief sparkle of accord between them and return to team lead mode.

That was just as it should be. But deep inside, Linn felt a little disappointed. The leather skirt was obviously just a skirt, and Tessa's premonitions nothing more than an urge to get Linn to spend some money.

Or were they?

Over the next hour, as she sat beside him on the couch, Kellan worked his way through the box of files, pointing out people and strategies and filling in the skeleton of the org chart with living, breathing criminals with rap sheets and families and networks of contacts. But every so often, when he thought she was absorbed in making notes in her notebook, out of the corner of her eye she'd catch him looking sideways at her.

She'd managed to keep the conversation so far almost completely on business, despite her Caroline persona's best efforts to derail it. This was a briefing, and he'd responded heroically, really. He hadn't so much as made a remark in response to Caroline's needling.

He was controlling himself admirably. Except for his eyes. There was no doubt there what he was thinking. That dark-chocolate gaze lingered and seemed to spark hot spots wherever it touched her.

She was playing with fire here. And why? For the sake of the job?

*Yeah, right,* her conscience scoffed. *The man walks on the wild side, and you like it. You've never dated a dangerous guy like this in your life. Oh, no. That would mean giving up control, wouldn't it? And we can't have that in our love life, can we?*

It wasn't about control. It was about partnership between equals.

*You've had it your way for too long. But you can't control this one. You can barely control yourself when you're around him. He pushes you, and that's what you like, isn't it?*

"So," she said calmly, silencing the voice, "that means that these two dealers get their product from you. How do you manage to stay uninvolved in the buys?"

His gaze traveled slowly up the front of her shirt, as if he were mentally doing up the buttons one by one, until it reached her face. "What?"

"The buys," she repeated, trying to remember what she'd just said. "How do you stay out of them? Do you have a couple of people do the carrying for you?"

"Tell me the real reason why you acted as Caroline tonight." His eyes had become hot and focused, and she knew the voice of her conscience was right. She did not have the upper hand here.

Not at all.

"To get into character," she said.

"You could do that on your own."

"No, I couldn't. I need you." That didn't come out right. "To play from."

"Do you?" His smile was molten, wicked. "You want to know what I think? I think you like being her. I think it gives you an excuse to be a bad girl."

"I don't need an excuse. I—"

"Then why so restrained all the time? Why not turn yourself loose once in a while?"

*Because then I'd be like my mother.*

"I can turn myself loose," she said a little defiantly. "I just don't get a lot of time to practice."

"How much practice do you want?" He turned and touched her just above her knee, where her skin was cool and bare under the heat of his hand. "What parts of Caroline do you want help with?"

Oh, God. He wasn't talking about deportment here. "The accent. The attitude. The, um…"

"Sexiness?" His hand slid a little farther up her leg, and she realized the leather miniskirt had been doing its job all along. In fact, it had scooted so far up her thighs that it was clear the damn thing was playing a come-hither game with his hand.

Maybe Tessa had been right about it after all.

"Kellan, please." She wasn't begging. She wasn't. She was trying to make her body stop wanting this.

He leaned in as if to say something quietly in her ear, but instead he tasted the skin just below her jaw. "Please what?"

"This isn't right."

Despite her words, her head rolled helplessly to meet his mouth. That wonderful mouth that made her think of sex and sin, that whispered bad things in her ear. Bad things she shouldn't want, but did. Other people broke the rules and took risks, but not her.

Not until now.

"I'm Dean, remember? Caroline doesn't work for me." The words hovered over her lips and she realized that he was waiting.

For her move. Her call.


As Caroline's—Linn's—he couldn't tell and didn't care any more. As her mouth opened and she reached up in invitation, Kellan threw his sensible resolve to keep this meeting businesslike straight out the window. His fingers slid up her leg to her hip, and he pulled her closer. In response, her arms wound around his neck. Her mouth was hot and demanding, though why that should surprise him he didn't take the time to speculate.

He stroked her tongue with his own, and she made a little noise in her throat. She tasted of wine and the scent of lime teased his nose again, as though a rise in her body temperature had released it. His own temperature was rising—no doubt about it.

Her lips were so soft, her tongue so welcoming, he fell into the kiss as though there would be no end to it.

Her head tilted back, and he released her mouth. Her throat was exposed for a second, and he lowered his head to see if the skin where her neck met her shoulder was as soft as it looked.

"Kellan," she whispered.

"Mmm?" It was. He kissed her throat, drawing in the scent of her.

"We can't do this."

"Yes, we can. You said so. We need the practice."

"It isn't practice."

He raised his head, confused, and met her troubled blue eyes. Then, dimly, he heard a cricket chirp.

The sound hardly registered. He had been enjoying her kisses and her skin, and he could have sworn she had been enjoying it, too, and now the spell was broken.

The cricket chirped again. Under the couch. "I think that's your phone." She pulled away.

His phone?

He tried to disconnect from the clash of desire and

disappointment. The only phone he carried these days was the one Tricky Ricky had the number for.

"Shit!"

He scrabbled through the pile of paper and files to find his jacket. He yanked the little cell phone out of the front pocket and practically pushed his thumb through the button.

"Yeah?"

"What's the matter? Bad time?" Rick O'Reilly sounded as if he hoped it were.

"Really bad time."

"You're breathing hard, guy. Don't tell me. You ran up a flight of stairs. Or could the lovely Caroline have something to do with it?"

For a moment Kellan felt reality and fantasy collide as the two worlds he inhabited overlapped. Caroline sprawled on the couch beside him, her lips swollen and parted, looking at him with a mixture of frustration and regret.

If O'Reilly had been in the room, he would cheerfully have choked him. "Screw you, man."

"I bet she wants to. I'm seeing her Saturday. Hope you don't mind."

Here's where Jealous Guy came in. "What?"

"Oh, she didn't tell you? She promised me she'd be careful. Careful and bad."

"You looking for a showdown or something, Rick? Because I'm not into that. I don't compete. If she wants to amuse herself with you because I got something else going, that's up to her."

"Oh, I'll amuse her, all right. Just don't expect her

around for breakfast Sunday morning. Or Monday morning, either."

"Is that what you called about? To tell me you were going to take my girlfriend to bed?"

"Pretty much. Thought it was only fair to be aboveboard. Since we're friends and all."

Linn leaned over and plucked the cell phone from his hand. "Hey, what—"

"Rick?" she purred into the phone. "Yes, it's me." Her lashes flicked up and her eyes held Kellan's gaze. "What do you think we were doing? No, actually, I'd just made him go out and get me a pint of lovely Ben and Jerry's ice cream." She laughed at something he said. "Cherry Garcia is my favorite, too…. Yes, darling, I'm sure you could, but I prefer something hot between my legs."

Kellan stared at her. How in the hell could she go from what she'd been doing with him to saying stuff like this to slimeball Rick O'Reilly?

"Darling, I'm assuming we're still on for tomorrow night? Just wanted to check. See you then." She made kissy noises into the phone and snapped it shut.

Her body seemed to lose all of its spine and seductiveness as she wilted into the cushions.

"Nothing like a call from Tricky Ricky to make you lose the moment." He tried to diffuse the awkwardness with a joke. She threw the cell phone limply in his direction, and he caught it. "I was having a pretty good moment. You can practice kissing with me anytime."

She rolled her head to look at him. "That's what it was, right? Practice for the job. You were kissing

Caroline." All trace of the sultry English accent had gone, and all that was left was a definite morning-after taste.

"Sure. We were rehearsing for tomorrow night. Getting comfortable with each other's part."

She looked pale and tired, and he'd kissed off all her lipstick. She also looked confused, as though she hadn't wanted him to agree with her.

Maybe some moments shouldn't be recaptured. Maybe he should just leave well enough alone. He shifted on the couch and began to gather up the files, leaving Rick O'Reilly's personal file out on the coffee table.

"Thanks for dinner. I'm going to head out. Maybe write up a report about his call while it's fresh in my mind."

He'd liked kissing her way too much, and his excuse that it was a rehearsal was transparent.

She stood up, pushing the skirt down with both hands. One of her feet was bare. She looked around a little helplessly, then gave up and kicked off the remaining sandal.

When he took his boxes out to the truck, he didn't let himself look back. He didn't want to see Investigator Linn Nichols looking vulnerable. He didn't want to know what her mom painted or what kinds of flowers were in her garden. Because if he wasn't careful, he'd find himself back inside, taking her in his arms for reasons that had nothing to do with Caroline or sex or the job.

And that was something he wasn't prepared for.

That call had reminded him it was all too easy to let it happen—those moments he hated when the line between Kellan and Dean blurred and he lost his grip on who he was supposed to be.

One way to prevent that was to remember who Caroline was. She was sex and danger and allure. She was the one he was allowed to want.

Not Linn.


ALL LINN WANTED was to crawl under the covers and hide, but there was one more thing she had to do tonight. She punched the pillow up against her back, picked up the phone and hit the number two on auto dial.

"Hey, Linn," her sister said instead of what most people would say, which was "hello."

"I *know* you have caller ID."

"I don't, honest. I just knew it was you."

"Yeah, sure."

"Are you okay, sweetie? You sound all…depressed or wrung out or something."

"Let's go with option B. Wrung out. It's just been a really long day."

"Is it the job? I can imagine it's a lot tougher environment than Santa Rita."

Close enough. "Yes. Look, I need a favor."

"Sure. What?"

"I need a pair of red high heels. You have any?"

There was a moment of silence in which Linn could imagine her sister sitting straight up in surprise, and she braced herself.

"You want to borrow a pair of my shoes? You're kidding. Red high heels are serious stuff. Who is he?"

"Why does it have to involve a guy? I'm working an operation and I have to wear this hooker outfit and need a pair of shoes. Okay? Simple as that."

"Linn Alexandra Nichols, it's never as simple as that. I know there's a man in this somewhere. I threw the cards for you yesterday, and the Emperor came up."

"Tess, give me a break. I can't deal with this stuff right now. Do you have a pair of shoes or not?"

"Linn, just listen to me for a minute. This is important."

It was the skirt all over again. Tessa wouldn't give up until she'd had her say, and like Harry Potter's red Howler envelopes, it only got worse the longer you put it off.

"All right." With a sigh, Linn pushed her hair out of her face. She wore it loose when she played Caroline and she'd been so disoriented when Kellan had left that she hadn't thought about tying it up again. "What does the Emperor have to tell me?"

"It means that an influential person has entered your life, but there's stuff going on that affects whether you can have a relationship or not. You should back off, because what you want personally has to take second place to business."

Linn had closed her eyes in sheer exhaustion. Now they flew open. "What?"

"I'm not done yet. You promised you'd listen."

"What do you mean, what I want has to take second place to business? Who says I want the guy, anyway?"

"I'm just telling you what the cards say. You have to figure out what they mean. Are you going to let me finish?"

Linn lay back. "Go ahead. I can hardly wait."

"Okay, the Emperor was in the Situation position. The Star was in the Love position."

"So what does that mean? I have stars in my eyes?"

"Linn."

"All right, all right. Star in the Love position."

"It's how you perceive yourself in love and relationships. But in this position it means your personal identity within the relationship right now."

Linn's scalp prickled. What personal identity? She had two at the moment. And only one of them had a tendency to wear black lace and kiss men who could get her into trouble. Maybe the cards could be more specific about just whose personality they were referring to.

"It points to your self-image, not how somebody else sees you," Tessa explained.

"My self-image?" She knew how Kellan saw her. But that wasn't how she saw herself. Or was it? This was really weird and mixed up and annoying. "Tess, I'm tired. Can we wrap this up?"

"Okay, okay. Bottom line is that you need to think about some aspect of yourself that needs development."

Her love life needed development, that was for sure. Since the departure of Jordan the Jerk a couple of months ago, about whom she'd made the mistake of being moderately serious, there hadn't been anyone. Most men outside law enforcement couldn't tolerate a woman with a badge…well, except for Mark, who'd been fonder of her handcuffs than he had been of her. She'd narrowed her pool of possibilities and started dating cops from other departments, who at least could understand double shifts and night work, but even there she'd run up against alpha types who couldn't tolerate strength in a woman.

Maybe with Caroline in the picture, she'd have better luck.

"One more," Tessa said.

"Thank God. I need to brush my teeth."

"I turned up Four of Swords in the Challenges position. That means you're on the cutting edge where you can turn challenges into a win/win situation with a bit of creativity and a positive attitude. Unlike what you're showing me here."

"Sorry. But this is just too weird for me."

"Even if it's accurate?"

"Lucky guesses. Vague pronouncements you can take to mean anything you want."

"Of course it's only relevant to you. One last thing."

"Shoot."

"The Four of Swords means you need to think about how you behave in recurring patterns. And it also means you need to get back to the cave. Take a bit of time off to evaluate and find your strength again."

"The swords have obviously never held down a job with CLEU. I'm in the middle of an operation. Taking a couple of days off isn't possible right now."

"I'm just telling you," Tessa said stubbornly. "Do with it what you will."

"Well, thanks for all the time you spent, anyhow. So about the shoes?"

"Of course you can borrow them. I have a pair of red stilettos that'd go perfectly with a hooker dress."

"Deal. I'll run over and pick them up tomorrow. 'Night."

"Good night, Linn. Give my regards to the Emperor."

Very funny, Linn thought as she turned off the phone and lay back on her bunched-up pillow. Tessa's idea of a joke.

She pulled her down comforter up over her head, but it was a long time before the images in her mind would let her sleep.

# 6

SHE WAS A HARD-NOSED investigator, Linn reminded herself as she walked into the office at the beginning of swing shift the next day. One of the best, according to the letter that had come six weeks ago and offered her a job with CLEU. She knew better than to get hot and bothered with the men she worked with, never mind her own team lead.

The recurring thought made her want to spend the day in solitude. Maybe she could volunteer for a couple of hours of surveillance to get her out of the office. Or even better, maybe the Santa Rita PD hadn't replaced her yet. Female officers were getting easier to come by, but not in narcotics. And she'd been good. They'd take her back in a minute—her lieutenant had said so during her exit interview.

No. She sat at her workstation and regarded the pile of reports stubbornly. She'd never go back, because that would mean admitting defeat. Admitting she hadn't been good enough, that she was too small for the big time.

Not gonna happen. Uh-uh. If there was one recurring pattern in her life, it was that she didn't accept failure.

It was only a kiss, really. She wasn't going to scuttle her career because of a kiss. She liked sex as much as the next woman—just ask Jordan the Jerk— but she had a brain to go with it. If that kiss was any indication, sex with Kellan Black would be every- thing his wicked smile promised. But she couldn't count on promises. He might send her body into ec- stasy and the very next morning send her file up to Internal Affairs.

She'd made a mistake in letting her Caroline side start something her Linn side couldn't finish. The thing to do now was damage control, and in her case, that meant not only fooling Rick O'Reilly, it meant wowing him. Getting everything she could out of him while giving nothing away, and handing it all to her team on a silver platter.

She could do that. She was a pro. And this time she wasn't going to forget it.

Satisfied with her internal pep talk, Linn fired up her computer and got down to prepping for the eve- ning's operation at the hotel.

A knock on the metal trim of her cube about twenty minutes later made her look up.

"Hey." Danny Kowalski motioned toward her guest chair. "Mind if I come in?"

"Help yourself. *Mi casa es* the State's *casa* and all that."

Kowalski looked like Hugh Jackman in his long- hair-with-beard phase, and according to one of the admins she'd talked to in the break room, he had the highest arrest record on the team. From the admin's tone, she wouldn't have minded one bit if Danny had arrested her.

"In the old building we used to have real offices with doors." He looked around the cube, as if she might have done something to change it.

"Yeah, they probably got too suspicious about what you were doing with the exhibits in there."

"No, fact was, the lieutenant got a little tired of the booby traps on his door. He figured with cubes at least he could see what everyone was up to."

She smiled, not at the actual words, but at his willingness to be companionable. He was the first of the team besides Kellan to actually approach her with more than a request for a surveillance or a report.

"So, are you settling in okay?" Danny leaned back in the chair.

"Yes. I was hoping for another fight poster. I could start a collection." Her grin told him she wasn't serious and wasn't bugged about their joke. Well, not now, anyway.

"I have connections. I could get you one."

"I bet. I suppose Kellan had nothing to do with it."

"Nah. We take our duty very seriously. Somebody has to keep him humble."

"You guys have been working together a long time, haven't you?"

"Three years. Max tour of duty is four, so we're looking at busting up our happy family soon."

Four years in narcotics. Many investigators she'd known hadn't lasted that long before they'd rotated out—burnout sometimes set in as early as two.

"He's a good lead." She tried to make it sound like an observation, not a question, and then wondered why she was pursuing it. Maybe Danny would think she was fishing for information because she was interested.

"Yeah, he is. Never asks us to do something he wouldn't go out there and do himself, no matter how much it stinks. He volunteered for this operation, you know." Danny crossed an ankle over his knee as if he were staying for a while. "Six months undercover. Some guys wait around to be assigned to stuff like that, but not him."

"He wants the Colombian pretty badly."

Danny nodded. "As do we all. Whoever he is, he's responsible for most of the cocaine supply in northern California. Shutting him down would be worth losing six months of your life. At least, Kellan thinks so."

"Does he have a family?" She couldn't seem to stop the words coming out of her mouth.

"His mom's a widow. His sisters are married, in Sacramento. I lost track of how many nieces and nephews he has. But if you're asking if he's married or anything, he's not."

Linn didn't like that speculative gleam in his eye. She kept her expression noncommittal. "It would be hard to maintain a relationship if you were in deep cover for months at a time. I was involved in an operation for a month with SRPD and that was hard enough."

"Boyfriend didn't like it?"

"You could say so. Jordan was a pilot. Let's just say the skies weren't quite so friendly after that."

Danny laughed. "Kell doesn't have to worry. He knows how to pick 'em. The female operators from the CLEU suboffices all over the State line up every time he finishes an op. It's like some kind of smoke signal goes up saying he's back in civvies, and the switchboard lights up like the Fourth of July."

"No kidding." Had the temperature dropped in her cube, or was it just the blood draining out of her head?

"I keep hoping he'll settle down and leave the field open for the rest of us, but so far it hasn't happened." He glanced at his watch. "Oops. I've got to go meet with a fink before we do the preop meeting. Nice talking to you."

"See you at six," she said faintly.

She turned back to her computer and stared blindly at the report on the screen.

Okay. Kellan was a short-term guy. She could deal with that. If anybody was short-term, it was Caroline. So Caroline was all he was going to get.

But she herself was a long-term girl. She'd had her share of men who didn't stick around, or who only called when they were in town. She was ready for more than that.

That one kiss they'd shared? That was it.

Their term was over.

ON A SCALE OF ONE TO TEN, the Dominion Hotel was about a five. Your husband could take you to dinner there. You'd book your cousins into a room there for a family wedding. You probably wouldn't take a client to the bar for a drink, though. It was noisy and crowded and, while it wasn't ideal for a business discussion, it was the perfect place for a meet. Linn had been there a couple of times on surveillance, but never as a private citizen. Given the choice of a night out in San Francisco, she'd pick a seafood dinner at the wharf and a stroll on the pier.

The team had met at the office for the six-o'clock briefing. She'd found them in a conference room—Kellan; Cooper Maxwell, who had a doctorate in psychology, which in her opinion was of no use whatsoever on the street unless the lowlifes wanted to talk about their feelings during buys; Danny Kowalski; and "Slim" Jim Macormick, who apparently had never met a lock he couldn't pick or, if the admins could be believed, a woman he couldn't seduce.

Her cover team, she thought, sinking into a chair at the end of the table. The men she depended on to save her life. The men who were trying not to look at her, probably because Kellan had already told them in graphic detail about his briefing with Caroline.

And they all had those damn caps on. Everyone had one but her. She slouched in the uncomfortable chair and resisted the urge to cross her arms and sulk.

"Here's the plan," their team lead said, and everyone stopped talking and swiveled in their chairs to give him their attention. "We're not going to wire Linn tonight."

"Why not?" Cooper wanted to know. "Why give up the evidence?"

Kellan shook his head. "I've seen what Linn will be wearing. You couldn't get a credit card under it, much less a recorder."

"No kidding." Maxwell looked as if he'd just been told it was Christmas. "Can you get underwear under it?"

Kellan grinned and shook his head, and Cooper sat back. "I love this job."

Linn shot him a look that scissored the grin from his face, and he had the grace to look chastened. These guys obviously had a steep climb up the learning curve when it came to working with a female investigator.

"Right. Linn, we'll drop you a block from the hotel and get settled in the bar. If he's already there, one of us will call your cell phone and give you a description of clothing and so on. He knows what you'll be wearing, but no need to give him an advantage."

"And where will you be?" she made herself ask. She'd rather not speak to him at all. Credit card, indeed. He'd made her buy the damn dress.

"I'll be in the back at the pay phone. There's a pretty good view back there, and it's dark."

She'd concentrated on making careful notes and had merely nodded.

After the briefing she'd gone home to change into

the red dress, and now here she was, walking along this street near Union Square, with every breeze in town trying to get under it.

She'd be lucky if it were just the breezes.

Her cell phone rang when she was about twenty yards from the portico of the hotel, and she dug it out of her purse.

"Yes?" said Kensington W8.

"It's me," Kellan replied. "He's got a table in the rear right corner. Khaki-colored silk suit, collarless shirt. Diamond stud, left ear. Fending off cruising boy toys as we speak."

"Lovely. And what about my boys?"

"All set up. Coop and Jim are at the table next to him pretending to be a couple."

"I'll buy a ticket to see that."

"There are no empty tables because the band's getting ready to start, so just go to the bar. I'm betting he'll come and get you."

"Will do." She flipped the phone shut without saying goodbye, took a deep breath and allowed an exiting patron to hold the door for her.

She felt the thump of the music under her ribs long before she entered the bar to a blast of sound and color and movement. She was going to have to sit in Tricky Ricky's lap and scream in his ear to make herself heard.

Tessa's red stiletto heels changed the way she walked, and her hips swayed gently as she made her way over to the bar.

"Buy you a drink, beautiful?" someone wanted to know as she passed a table.

"Looking for company?" asked another man as she laid her evening bag on the bar.

"Thank you, no," she told him, and turned to the bartender. "Chardonnay, please."

The wine appeared with magical speed, and as it did, she felt a hand slide up her bare back from waist to shoulder blade.

"I love a bad girl in red."

She controlled the reflex in her right arm that would have decked him with an elbow to the chin, and turned slowly.

"Richard?"

Raw-silk suit, flawlessly cut. Diamond stud. The coldest blue eyes she'd ever seen above a nose that had been broken at some time in the past. Square face, smiling. Shoulders that belonged to an ex-football player. Hadn't worked out in a while, but still more than a female operative without extensive martial arts training could safely take on in a fight.

Rick O'Reilly in the flesh.

"I love the way you say that. Damn, but you are hot."

Her lashes dropped and then swept upward slowly, provocatively, until she met his gaze. "You make me sound like something illegal."

"I hope you are. Come on. I have a table."

He picked up her wine and she followed him to the rear of the room, out of the direct range of the speakers, where it was marginally quieter. When he held a chair for her, she seated herself, crossed her legs and took her glass.

He sat down in the chair that put his back to the wall. To her left, gazing soulfully into each other's eyes, were Cooper and Jim. She resisted the dual urge to laugh and to scan the room for Kellan, and wondered how long he'd give her with the target before he came over and played Jealous Guy.

"So Dean let you out to play, did he?" O'Reilly looked her over with approval, as if she were something he'd just spent a fortune on.

"I told you on the phone there was no 'let,'" she replied coolly. "I'm simply here for a visit. Dean and I have been friends for a long time, but he doesn't own me."

"Friends?"

"Yes. Very good friends."

"You're sleeping with him."

"Of course." She managed to sound a little surprised that he would ask. "What girl wouldn't?"

"A girl who was sleeping with me." He leaned over and ran one finger over the back of her hand. "You can bet you wouldn't be going out with other people. I know how to keep a woman satisfied."

"So I understand." She slanted him a look over her wineglass that implied his prowess was legendary. From the corner of her eye she saw Jim bury a grin in his glass of beer.

"What do you mean? Who have you been talking to?"

"Why, you, darling. Didn't you tell me you had a

little something in your bedroom? And I don't mean…" She flicked a lazy glance at his crotch.

He leaned back in his chair. "You're a fast worker, aren't you? Not before we get to know each other real well first."

She shrugged and sipped her wine.

"I can show a lady a good time without any extras, you know." He sounded a little defensive.

"I'm sure you can. But I find it adds to the experience."

"So, what, you don't play without it?"

She smiled and held his gaze. "There would have to be quite an incentive." *Think you're man enough to have sex with me without drugs?*

If he had been a bullfrog, he would have swelled up. As it was, he put down his glass and skewered her with that hard blue gaze.

"I'll give you incentive. As soon as we—"

"You know, O'Reilly, I didn't think you'd go through with it."

Linn and the drug dealer looked up at the same time. Kellan Black stood over them, his arms crossed so that his silk dress shirt pulled tight around the bunched muscles in his arms, looking as if he'd like to start a fight then and there.

O'Reilly grinned. "Dean. Since when have I ever backed away from a challenge?"

"I don't remember any challenge. Mind if I join you?"

"Yeah."

"Too bad." He pulled a chair over from Cooper

and Jim's table and straddled it. His glance at Linn held resentment. "Having fun, baby?"

She smiled at him.

"I thought when you came all the way over from England that you'd be spending time with me."

"I have been spending time with you, darling. We've been in bed for two days."

"So, what, now you're bored and want to see the sights? You could have said something, and I'd have taken you out."

She slid a glance at O'Reilly that practically smoldered. "You said you were busy. And Richard made me an offer I couldn't refuse."

"He did, did he? And what would that be?"

"That's between me and Caroline," O'Reilly put in.

"Get that smug look off your face. At least you could have taken her to the St. Francis or something, not this two-bit dive."

"It was convenient."

Linn saw Cooper straighten. Did that mean O'Reilly's safe house was somewhere near here? Maybe even within walking distance? If so, tailing him would be simple.

But investigations were never that simple. For all they knew, he could be hiding across the Bay in Oakland and all he meant was that the hotel was close to a train station.

"Yeah, well, I'm glad this is convenient for you. Carrie, honey, come on. It's time to go."

She raised an eyebrow. "I'm with Richard at the moment, love."

He stared at her, plainly flummoxed. "You spend two days in the sack with me and now you're with someone else? Just like that?"

"I came to visit you, Dean, darling. Not marry you."

"Yeah," O'Reilly put in. "You don't have any claim on her. And like she said, I made her a better offer."

Kellan looked from one to the other. "What does that mean?"

O'Reilly fingered the inner pocket of his jacket, where his cigarettes probably were. But there was no smoking indoors in California, even in a bar. "Maybe it's something you want."

Kellan leaned over and spoke in low, threatening tones. "You've been stalling for a week. I want that introduction. The money's ready to go. Do it now or don't do it at all."

O'Reilly grinned, and his gaze returned to Linn, sliding down her throat and stalling on the front of her dress. "Let's see if your lady can convince me. Somewhere other than here."

# 7

"SHE'S NOT GOING anywhere with you," Kellan said flatly. It wasn't just an act. He meant it. It was too risky to have her go to an unknown, unsecured location with their target. Any time Linn spent with O'Reilly had to be on CLEU's terms, carefully monitored, with surroundings as safe as they could make them for the operator. Which meant Linn had to call the shots and make O'Reilly do what she wanted.

Here was where he hoped he'd read her right. That she wouldn't work outside the lines, but that she knew an operator's territory well enough to stay strictly inside it.

"Dean, really," Caroline—Linn, dammit—purred. "I'll decide, thank you."

"Fine." He waved his hands as if shedding all responsibility. "Do what you want. Just don't expect me to give you a place to stay when you're done. In fact, you know what?" He glared at O'Reilly. "Why don't you just tell me where your little love nest is, and I'll send her stuff over for you."

O'Reilly grinned, evidently pleased he'd managed to get under Dean's skin for once. *The address,* Kellan urged him silently. *Give me your safe house so we can raid it and get something on the Colombian.*

"Depends on whether I decide to keep her for a week. I'll let you know after tonight."

Abruptly, Linn pushed her wine away and stood, giving Kellan an eyeful of those legs and sky-high shoes. "This is ridiculous." Coldly, she looked at both of them. "Keep me, indeed. The pair of you are more interested in your little territorial fights than in what I want. I don't need that."

She sounded so royally, Britishly pissed off. Not to mention the woman was hot as hell when she was angry. She spun on one four-inch heel and stalked away, if that figure-eight sway of her beautiful rear end could be called stalking.

"That is one fine woman," O'Reilly said. "Too bad you're going to lose her to me." He tossed a twenty on the table and took off after her.

Kellan exchanged a glance with Coop and Slim. "Lobby," Coop said.

"She doesn't get in his car."

"Right."

The cover team stayed out of sight when they caught up to Linn and O'Reilly, who were standing at the bottom of the staircase that led to the mezzanine floor. Linn looked imperious, and O'Reilly, for all his size and power in the underworld, looked as though he were begging.

Kellan would give a week's pay to know what

they were saying, because it probably wasn't going to go in her report.

Finally it looked as though they had come to some kind of agreement. O'Reilly slipped an arm around her and they walked out the front door, but not before Kellan saw his hand dip into the deep V of the back of her dress, and slide around her waist—inside the fabric.

Adrenaline prickled into his veins. He was going to kill the rat. She wasn't wearing a bra. O'Reilly could cop a feel on the way down the front steps and there wouldn't be anything anybody could do about it.

Kellan didn't take the time to analyze why another man's hands on Linn's body infuriated him. The cover team's first priority was to get out on the street and make sure she was safe. And that meant preventing her from getting into his car.

Kellan approached the front door in time to see O'Reilly flag a taxi and put Linn into it.

Alone.

The cab signaled and pulled out into traffic, and Kellan yanked his cell phone out of his pocket, flipping the switch that made it a walkie-talkie.

"You and Slim stay with O'Reilly," he told Coop. "I'm going to debrief Nichols. We need to know if she's set up another meet with him, and how soon."

"Four," Coop said, using an abbreviated form of the ten code, and disconnected.

Victor-21 was parked a block away. Kellan gambled that she'd go home instead of back to the office in that dress and those shoes and drove down the peninsula to San Mateo as fast as he dared. He still didn't beat her crazy cab driver, who must have been doing forty miles over the limit.

She answered his knock so quickly she must have just closed the door. "Kellan." Her voice held surprise. "What are you doing here?"

"Debriefing." He shouldered past her without an invitation and swung the door closed. "You all right?"

"Of course." She looked a little puzzled at the urgency in his tone. "I was going to have a drink. Want one?"

"What are you drinking?"

"Baileys."

He grimaced. "I'll have a beer if you have it."

She brought him a beer and took a sip of the brown stuff in her glass. "I'll just be a second. I have to get out of these clothes. Every draft in San Francisco is trying to get in. I was freezing all night."

"That wasn't all that got in."

"What?" She put her drink on the table and looked at him from across the room.

"I saw where O'Reilly's hands were when you went out the door." He needed to do something. Brief her. Kiss her. Fight with her. Anything to dissipate the adrenaline coursing through his system.

She made a face. "Oh, that. Well, when a guy can't get what he wants, he takes what he can have."

He put his beer down. "And he can have you?"

"Are you still being Dean?"

Did he really sound that jealous? "No, I'm me." Suddenly he didn't care how he sounded. "So you let the target cop a feel?"

She tilted her head and gave him a quizzical look. "What's it to you if I did? I was working. Playing a part."

"Did you like it?"

"Kellan, what is the matter with you? Of course I didn't like it. He's a slimy creep. But it was my job to make him want to see me again, so I did."

"So you let him touch you."

She rolled her eyes. "Yes, and now I need to take a shower. Happy?"

With that, she turned away and walked off down the hall. Kellan slouched into the colorful cushions on the couch and rubbed his face with both hands. This was what he got for spending too much time in a role. Jealousy? Because a lowlife touched his imaginary girlfriend? How twisted was that? If he were a real leader, he'd be concerned about her well-being and safety instead of lecturing her about where she'd let O'Reilly put his hands. Guilt prodded him off the couch and he followed the sound of the shower down the darkened hall.

"Linn?"

"What?" she said from inside the bathroom.

"Can I talk to you?"

"Kellan can talk to me. Dean can go take a hike." Her voice sounded muffled, as if water were cascading down her face and she was trying to talk through closed lips.

Okay, so it was a little strange to do a debrief through a bathroom door, but if she was willing to let him, after the debacle of the previous night, he'd do it.

The door hadn't quite latched. He leaned against the wall and spoke into the open crack, doing his best not to think about hot water and soap and this woman's beautiful body.

"So what did you get on O'Reilly's plans?"

"He wants to arrange a weekend together." The water splashed and hissed. This was a bad idea. He should have waited until she was dressed and back out in the living room.

"Some kind of house party up in the wine country," she went on. "You, me, some friends of his, and, quote, a friend who owns the vineyard, unquote. You can see why I was concentrating more on getting information out of him than where his damn hands were."

She had a point. "He said that? This friend owns the vineyard? The Colombian is supposed to own property in California."

"So your file said." The water shut off, and he straightened. In a moment he heard the shower door slide open.

*Step away from the door.*

But his feet didn't move. Instead he stood in the dim hallway, and listened to the quiet, intimate sounds she made. The quick brush of a towel making its way down her body. The soft *flump* of a robe settling on her shoulders. The emphatic rustle of a belt being knotted. A little cloud of steam puffed out of the half inch of space that allowed him to hear but not see.

He couldn't remember the last time he'd slowed down enough to simply stand and listen. In his experience, a shower was either a quick necessity or an excuse for wet sex. But strangely, he didn't want to barge in there and try to get something going with her. He was just content to stand outside the door and talk, to experience the odd intimacy that was usually the result of living with someone. Not that he'd ever done that.

Not successfully, anyway. He'd tried it once or twice over the years, back when he'd believed that loving someone meant practical little things like finding a place to live together, trusting each other, thinking more than a weekend ahead. But both times he'd come back to find his partner gone, physically the first time—though she'd left a nice note—and emotionally the second time. A natural reaction, Donna had said defensively as she'd packed her boxes, to his never being there when she needed him.

Well, trusting someone to be there when you got back was a little harder than it sounded, too. He wondered if Linn had the same problems.

*Go back to the living room.*

This time, his feet seemed inclined to obey, but before he'd taken more than a step away, she spoke again.

"How do I get out of spending that much time with him?"

"Maybe you don't." His voice was lower, now that he didn't have to communicate through the sound of water. He leaned on the wall and continued to speak through the opening. "This could be it. Maybe it's a stretch to think the Colombian will actually show. Maybe O'Reilly's just jerking our chain. He's done it before. But if it's real and he does plan to introduce me, we need to be ready."

In the silence, several small sounds told him she was running a comb through her wet hair. "Kellan?"

"Yeah?"

"Do you normally debrief people while they're in the shower?" The door swung open and she stood there, her hair slicked away from her face, her skin scrubbed and rosy. A cloud of steam scented with lime touched his face. She wore a dark-green terry robe, so soft and thick his fingers would probably disappear into it if he put his hands on her shoulders. The robe concealed everything from neck to ankles and made her look about seventeen.

"That's why you smell like limes," he said inanely. "The soap."

"You should go into police work." He was sure she meant to be flip, but the words came out a little too breathlessly.

He tried to focus on the briefing, but instead he seemed to be focusing on the hollow in her throat, which was all that the robe allowed him to see. "Did he say anything more about this friend?" he asked with an effort.

"Not much. But the tone of his voice was different. As if he had a secret and was trying to keep it back."

"These guys don't confide in women. Hint, lie, confuse, but not confide."

"I haven't met many that do," she agreed. "Kellan?"

"Yes?"

"Why are we standing in the bathroom door?"

He thought for a second. "Because I like the smell of limes?"

That was only part of it. He liked seeing her this way, in her own environment, without the protection of the businesslike clothes she wore or the shell of the tough State agent that she created with words and actions. He liked the sense of peace and near intimacy. They'd actually managed to get through an entire ten-minute conversation without antagonism.

"You do?"

"Let me rephrase that." He leaned in and took a deep breath. "I like the smell of limes on *you*."

THE CONSTRICTION in her chest told Linn she'd stopped breathing, and she dragged air into her lungs—air that was filled with the scent of her soap and hot skin and a whiff of something that had to be Kellan's cologne. It was a delicious mixture, and threatened to go straight to her head.

His lips touched the side of her neck, as gentle as a question, and she shivered at the contact.

This was different, somehow, from when he'd kissed her the other night and tried to convince them both that it was practice for getting into their parts. Maybe it had been. Or maybe she was just far too susceptible to him and she didn't care whether it was practice or not.

Because this gentleness was undoing her even faster than passion could. He knew she was undressed and vulnerable, and the hallway was dark. Their voices had been low and intimate. Was that it? Was the siren call of intimacy making her respond to him in a way she hadn't the other night?

His mouth had reached her ear now, taking her earlobe tender prisoner and touching it with his tongue. She shivered again, unable to help herself.

"Are you cold?" he whispered.

"No." On the contrary, her body temperature jumped a couple of degrees every time his mouth moved.

There was something sexual and elemental in him that called to the corresponding part of her that she'd buried in her fight to succeed. That part of her was hungry and reckless and wanted to embrace the bad boy, to take the risk, to say to hell with the consequences as long as they could find satisfaction in each other.

But what about him? What had made him come to her house and stand in the dark talking to her while she showered? What element in her would make *him* take the risk? Because he had the most to lose in their working relationship. He was the one in charge. Was it only the dangerous, sexual Caroline that attracted him? Or something else?

Suddenly she had to know, before this went any further.

"Kellan," she whispered just as his lips completed their leisurely exploration of her jaw and arrived at the corner of her mouth.

"Mmm?"

"Are you—"

But as her lips parted on the *you* he kissed the rest of her question into silence, and in the next second she forgot what she'd been going to say anyhow. His kiss was just as slow and sensual as it had been when she'd acted like Caroline. His mouth played over hers, coaxing, drawing her in, then stroking her tongue with his own as though they had all night to discover each other.

She slid her arms around his neck and pressed into the kiss, her thighs moving between his. Her hands touched his hair and settled on his shoulders, palms flat against a silk shirt that held the heat of his body. The robe parted halfway down, and the lightweight wool of his trousers, soft and a little scratchy, brushed the insides of her knees.

His hands settled around her waist. She felt a tug and then coolness as the tie fell away and her bathrobe opened all the way down the front.

Warm hands. Warm hands splayed on her ribs, then curved to follow the indent of her waist and the flare of her hips. His kiss changed angle, and she made a soft sound in her throat as it deepened and increased in urgency. Both of his hands slid up her rib cage as though he wanted to lift her, but instead, they slowed and, an inch at a time, moved to cover her breasts.

This time it was he who made a little sound, just before he broke the kiss. His hands felt wonderful as they cupped her flesh, soothing the ache, testing their fullness.

Her heart leaped in her chest as her brain caught up with her body and she realized what they were doing. She'd made no move to stop him. In fact, she didn't even want to—

A two-note beep and a burst of static came from the living room. "Victor-21?" asked a deep male voice.

Linn jumped back, grabbing both sides of the robe and clutching them together. "Who's that?" Had the team followed Kellan to her apartment? Was she about to be caught half-naked in the hallway by all the men she worked with?

Kellan made an exasperated noise. "It's Coop. On the phone. I forgot to turn off the walkie-talkie."

"Victor-21, you in service? Sierra-5."

With a sigh, he released her and went into the living room. She knotted the tie on her robe even more tightly than it had been before, and looked around the corner. He stood in front of the coffee table, his phone flipped open.

"Victor-21. Go."

"We're in pursuit," Coop said.

"Where's our target?"

"Not sure."

"What does that mean?"

"It means he gave the valet his ticket to get the car, but instead of waiting for it, he went into the dining room and took a table. By the time we got there and got set up, he'd gone to the men's. He never came back."

"You lost him?" The answer was so obvious that Linn hardly expected Cooper to reply. "So where did the valet go with his car?"

"Considering you told us to stay with the target, not his car, I couldn't tell you."

"He probably took it around back or something, and O'Reilly just went out through the kitchen."

"So how'd the debriefing go?" Cooper's tone was a little nettled.

Linn met Kellan's glance. "Looks like Dean and Caroline are going to be invited to a house party at some vineyard in the wine country. And get this— there may be an introduction to the guy who owns the property."

"You think it's the Colombian?"

"I don't know. Could be."

"When do we find out it's a go?"

"I'm riding O'Reilly about an introduction, and he wants to spend time with Caroline, so I'm betting it's soon."

"We're back to square one, waiting for him to call The Girl."

"Yep. Why don't you head back to the Dominion? See if you can persuade the valet to talk to us."

"Will do. Coming?"

Another glance at Linn. "Yeah."

He clicked off, then switched the little unit back to telephone mode and pocketed it. "Once again, duty calls."

She felt let down—frustrated—ready to push him backward onto the couch and climb on top of him, and he'd gone from lover back to cop as easily as if she hadn't been standing there.

"You should go, then." He was doing his job. It wasn't personal.

Yes, it was. It was getting too damn personal.

He made a movement toward her, but the look on her face must have stopped him. And then, before she could do anything to change it, he was gone.

# 8

LINN DRAINED THE LAST of the Baileys in her glass
and set it on the nightstand with a click. Tessa's red
shoes lay on the floor, one upright and one on its side.
Red shoes, dim lighting and chocolate. All the props
and not a man in sight.

There had been nothing else he could do, of
course. Kellan couldn't very well have said, "No, I'm
going to stay here and finish undressing Linn," now,
could he? And if he'd stayed more than a few minutes after agreeing to meet the other members of the
team, they'd have known something was up, and
they'd have asked questions. Before you knew it,
gossip about the two of them would be all over the
office.

She'd wanted him to stay. Call her a glutton for
punishment, call her reckless, but there was a reason
her brain had shorted out when he'd undone her robe.
She'd wanted him to do it. Had craved his kiss, had
practically climbed his legs trying to get closer.

And he'd known it.

Known it and left, anyway.

Abruptly, Linn swung her legs off the bed and

hooked two fingers through the straps of the shoes. She needed to get them out of her room. The shower had taken care of the memory of O'Reilly's hands on her skin, but nothing would erase the feel of Kellan's mouth on hers or the way her body had responded to his hands.

Tessa might have her idiosyncrasies, but she was still willing to dish the dirt late at night. Linn would run the shoes over to her and get her mind off Kellan Black.

At the lobby door of Tess's apartment building, Linn reached to push the buzzer. But before she touched it, the door clicked open. Maybe the system was malfunctioning.

Tess met her at the door of her third-floor apartment. "Hey."

"Sorry about coming over without calling first. You should tell the super about the front door. It just clicks and lets people in."

"No, it doesn't. I knew you were there."

"Oh, right. You magically knew it was me about to ring your buzzer, and not some psychotic with a blade in his pocket?"

"No." Tess grinned. "You need a new muffler. I heard you come up the street, and I can see the front walk from my window."

Linn had to laugh. "Okay. Debunk your own mystique. Here, I brought your shoes."

"Did they work?"

"They got the job done. I sure wouldn't want to run for my life in them, though."

"They're not made for running, silly." Tess leaned

in the bedroom door and tossed the shoes inside, then came back into the kitchen. "They're made for catching."

"Believe me, the only catching I want to do is my target."

"Not the Emperor?" Tessa reached for the kettle to make a cup of the boiled grass and seed pods she called tea. Linn drank it out of love because she knew Tess liked the stuff.

"Who's the Emperor?" Linn asked, as if she didn't know. State regulations said she shouldn't have let him into her house. But once she had, her own desire said she shouldn't have let him out of it.

"I think you know."

"All right, smart mouth. I do. He's my team lead."

Tess nodded, a wise woman in a ponytail and a San Jose Sharks hockey sweatshirt. "Uh-huh. That powerful guy for whom you have to put business before pleasure?"

Only Tess got her *who*s and *whom*s correct in her own kitchen. "That'd be him. You can add some honey if you want." If she had to drink liquid grass, at least she'd get some flavor out of it.

Tess handed her a mug and led the way over to the couch. "Since when does pleasure come into it, anyhow? I thought there were all kinds of rules against fraternizing among the troops."

"There are." Linn contemplated the pale-gold liquid in her mug. "Tons of them. And for good reason. But my problem is that I'm supposed to be playing this guy's girlfriend."

"Is that a bad thing?"

"No. You should see him. The guy is incredible."

"Single?"

"Yup."

"Straight?"

"Oh, yeah."

"Available?"

"So it would seem."

Tess tucked her legs beneath her. "It's simple. Right now is a bad time. But when the case is closed, you guys are both free to get together."

Linn pursed her mouth and took an experimental sip of her tea. *Yuck.* "It's complicated."

"The only complication I could see is if he had someone already. Or a bunch of kids by various mothers."

She may as well just come right out and say it. "He thinks I'm someone else. And the someone else is who he really wants to get together with."

Her sister's brows knotted. "Run that by me again? I thought you worked together. Had ID badges and all that. That should straighten him out pretty quickly, I would think."

Linn sighed. It sounded ridiculous when she put it into words. "I'm doing an undercover op playing a British jet-setter named Caroline. She's the one who wears red shoes and hooker outfits. The target wants to take her—me—away from Kellan and I'm supposed to use that. And Kellan—that's my team lead—has the hots for Caroline, too. He says we have to play like we're in a sexual relationship, and he keeps acting like we are. Coming on to me." She put her mug down, leaned her elbows on her knees, and sighed. Her fingers curled into her hair on either side of her head. "Making me absolutely crazy."

"Coming on to you, or you when you're playing Caroline?"

"Me when I'm playing Caroline." Except for tonight. Tonight had confused her all over again, because once she'd shed the red dress, she'd shed Caroline, too. And he'd still kissed her as though he'd meant to make love to her.

Linn's hands dropped to her thighs, and she leaned back into Tessa's squashy secondhand couch. "Most of the time we don't get along worth beans when I'm myself."

"How is that possible?" Tess's tone was full of wonder.

"Like this." Linn pulled the elastic band out of her hair, shook it out, and pulled Caroline on like a cloak. "I don't know who you're calling 'Emperor,' darling, but it's not my habit to allow a man that much control."

Tessa's eyes grew round. "Wow! How do you do that?"

Linn took a deep breath and felt her face tighten back to normal. Gathering up her hair, she pulled it into a ponytail and snapped the elastic around it. "I didn't even know I could, until this past Wednesday. A natural talent, I guess."

"I can't believe it. The eyes. The mouth. The boredom with the world. Not to mention the accent. It's amazing."

"Well, amazing or not, it's that person he wants to make love to. Not me. Which is good," she added hastily. "Getting involved with my team lead would totally screw up my chances in CLEU."

"That's what it means," Tess breathed. "The Star. When I did your cards."

"Tess, for God's sake, I'm trying to have a rational conversation here."

"No, no, just listen. In the Love position one of the meanings of the Star card relates to clarity about yourself. Remember I told you there was some aspect of yourself that needed development? Well, this is it!" She sat back, a plainclothes prophet, pleased with her own brilliance.

"I have no idea what you're talking about," Linn said flatly. "I think I'd better go. Thanks for the tea. And the shoes."

"Linn, you are so structured and ordered you don't even know there is a box, much less that you can think outside of it. This is where the creativity comes in. The aspect of yourself that needs development is *her.* Caroline. Your sexy self. Don't you see?"

"My ability to out-think lowlifes is what makes me succeed. I cross logic with intuition and it works. None of this weirdness where you pick definitions of people's lives out of cards like it was some big metaphysical lottery."

"Don't be mad at me, Linn. I'm trying to help. You need to exercise your sexual identity. Caroline is just an aspect of you that you've sublimated your whole life. Come on. When was the last time you actually had sex?"

"With Jordan the Jerk. And don't remind me."

"Sorry." Tessa made a face, but it was obvious she wasn't finished yet. "You know what I think? I think you don't trust anything that makes you get emotional. You picked Jordan because he's a robot who puts starch in his undies, and you had a built-in excuse to dump him. You have a hard time relating to Mom and Dad because they celebrate their emotional lives in paintings and books."

"One book."

"Don't quibble."

Not for the first time, Linn wondered how she'd landed in a family like this. When her parents weren't off finding their emotional selves in Israel or Nepal, they were hanging out in the Haight with friends and relatives who hadn't figured out that the sixties were over. If the truth had to be told, her big teenage rebellion had consisted of getting straight A's in school and going not to Berkeley or Santa Cruz, but to Stanford. And a career in law enforcement after that, just to spit in her father's eye.

"You can call it celebrating their emotional lives if you want," she said to Tessa. "I call it selfishness and irresponsibility."

"Why?" Tessa demanded. "They got us launched into the world. What's wrong with zooming around in a motor home if they feel like it?"

"Because they're not here for you and me. They've never been there for us...even when they were here."

Her sister gave her a long look. "You have a very different view of our childhood than I do."

"That's because you're like them!" The words popped out of her mouth before she could hold them back. She had nothing to lose, so she plunged on. "You do what you want, you say what you want, your emotions are right out there for everyone to see. Just like Mom's paintings. Don't you guys know how dangerous that is?"

"It's only dangerous if you let it be that way," Tessa said slowly. "If you don't trust the people around you. If you don't trust yourself to be an emotional woman, a sexy woman. Is that the problem, Linn? Here's this team lead of yours who wants to put your relationship on a whole other level and you don't trust him with that woman. You're running as fast as you can to get away."

"Not all the time," Linn confessed, driven to it by Tessa's uncanny knack for the truth. No wonder she was doing a degree in psychology. Climbing into people's heads and camping there seemed to be second nature for her.

Could Caroline really be an aspect of her sexual identity? No way could she trust that. She had proof that letting Caroline out of her cage for any reason but business was a bad idea. In fact, Caroline only needed to be on display when she, Linn, was with Rick O'Reilly. Working.

Because Tessa was right. She didn't trust that side of herself to stay away from the cliff edge of control where her family lived all the time. Anything else

might put her over that edge, and she needed to remember how high the risks were.

Especially as far as Kellan Black was concerned.

THE FIRST ORDER OF BUSINESS when the team met the
next day was Rick O'Reilly's house party and how
much security the team could provide for Linn and
Kellan if the invitation to the winery were real. After
sitting for two hours in the stuffy conference room
while everyone else debated strategies and decided on
equipment and surveillance coverage, the team finally
figured out that she had something to contribute, too.
They followed Linn down the hall to the glass interview room where the "hot number" waited. There was
nothing left to do now but confirm that the meet was
actually scheduled, and for that they needed Caroline.

Some of the investigators from the other teams
picked up the scent of potential entertainment and
left their cubicles to join them. Linn glanced up from
the phone, where she was attempting to get over
feeling left out and get into character.

"I'm going to charge you guys admission. Would
you back off?"

They just grinned and made themselves comfortable around the recording equipment. At least she'd
had a little experience at being Caroline now. More
than she ever wanted, and there was no end in sight.

Lieutenant Bryan stuck his head in the door,
speaking over his shoulder. "Black, you get in here
with her. You're supposed to be together. If he wants
to talk to you, you'd better be on hand."

Great. So much for being able to close her eyes and pretend the audience wasn't there.

Kellan strode to a chair and sat, tilting it back on its hind legs. He watched as she dialed the numbers of O'Reilly's latest cell phone, the number he'd slipped her last night during the meet at the Dominion Hotel.

She had two rings in which to become Caroline, but with Kellan in the room watching her it seemed easier. Particularly since he was looking at her with that intent gaze.

Complete concentration.

Her lover, watching her call another man.

The call clicked through. "Yeah?"

"Richard," she purred.

"Well, hello, babe. Couldn't even wait a day, could you?"

"I said I'd ring you back. And I always keep my promises."

"I'll hold you to that. You promised me a blow job, if I remember right."

Linn didn't even flinch at the knowledge that that remark had been recorded, the girls in the basement would transcribe it, and it would go on permanent record to be used as evidence in court. There were times when denial was a very useful skill.

"All in good time, darling. I'm calling about the invitation to your little house party."

"Yeah? You going to come?"

"If you were serious about it, I'd love to. Dean says the wine country is lovely, and of course I've never been."

"Unlike Dean, I don't waste a lot of time staring at the scenery. Napa's for business. It's my friend's place when he's in Northern Cal. He has a place in Miami, too, but sometimes it gets hot down there."

"I can imagine."

"He's invited us for Thursday through Sunday."

"I'll be there."

"No, I'll send a car for you. I treat a lady right."

"Dean, too?"

O'Reilly sighed noisily. "Yeah, Dean, too. But when you have a few days with me you'll dump that guy."

"You should really treat your customers better, darling."

"Oh, I am. He gets to meet my friend, we talk business, everybody's happy. But what's between you and me happens outside of that."

"And what is between you and me?"

"That blow job, for starters. And after that, whatever you want."

She laughed, low and inviting. "So Thursday morning, then? The limo?"

"Yeah. Where are you?"

Without missing a beat, she said, "At Dean's, of course," and gave him the address of CLEU's temporary location in the Marina district, where Dean had been seen entering and exiting often enough to give the impression he lived there.

"I'll send it for noon. See you up there, babe."

"I'll be ready for you, darling." She rang off, and the tape operator gave Bryan the thumbs-up. The woman punched another line and took the phone company's incoming call.

"We got a lock on his location." The operator's plastic nametag read Claire Bennet, Linn saw as she joined them.

"Do you want us to go?" Danny asked.

Bryan shook his head. "Nah, he'll be long gone. Where was he?" he asked Ms. Bennet.

"Looks like a gym. Wonderbodies, south of Market."

"We'll go with our original plan. For now, you guys better get ready for a trip. Kowalski and Maxwell, you're in the van. Macormick, you'll be in radio contact here. Black and Nichols, get yourselves down to the house. You've got a day to prep for this."

"I'm in court tomorrow," Linn remembered suddenly. "A Santa Rita case."

"Fine, but you'll stay at the house tomorrow night and let Black brief you as thoroughly as possible. If O'Reilly has half a brain, which I know he does, he'll have people around there Thursday morning. I want you looking like you're really staying there."

*And that Kellan Black lives there.*

Linn pushed the thought out of her mind. She was going to keep this whole operation on a businesslike basis if it killed her. The safe house had more than one bedroom and a couch besides. They could coexist just fine as long as he didn't kiss her or talk to her through the bathroom door or any of his other dangerous behaviors that made her knees and her resolve weaken. She'd tell him calmly and unemotionally that she wasn't prepared for anything but a business relationship.

Sure she would.

Just as soon as she came up with the strength to do it.

A DAY IN COURT in Santa Rita went a long way to restoring Linn's sanity and bringing her back to the real world of admissible evidence and sentencing and pleas. She returned to the SRPD building downtown afterward, to shoot the breeze with her former workmates and look up Natalie Wong.

The identification expert, whose specialty was the Automated Fingerprint Identification System, or AFIS for short, looked up from her screen and smiled in delight when Linn paused in the lab's doorway.

"Linn!" They hugged, and Nat stood back a little to look her over. "You've lost weight. But it looks like the big city suits you."

Linn shook her head and sank into the guest chair in front of Natalie's workstation. "I had to go through PT all over again. I worked out before, but not like this. I haven't had a butt this firm since I was twenty."

"Gee, a whole eight years ago. Give me a break." Natalie resumed her seat and tilted the chair as far as its ergonomically correct back would allow. "So, what's new?"

Linn rolled her eyes. "Where do I start?"

"I haven't had e-mail from you in a week. Something must be going on."

"I've been trying to survive at CLEU. It's not easy."

"You survived initiation here. Both of us did. CLEU can't be any worse."

"It's worse. At least here they didn't expect me to put on a red silk dress and seduce a drug runner."

Natalie blinked. "No kidding."

"And that's just the beginning. My team lead and I are playing a couple and we're supposed to go up to Napa to this house party and meet the person that we hope is the importer."

Natalie rocked forward and the mechanism under her chair made a thunking noise. "What's wrong with that? Sounds like a normal operation to me."

"I know what to do with the criminal, even though he thinks he's God's gift to women. It's my lead I'm concerned about."

"Why?"

"For starters, when he walks into a room it's way too easy to forget about the regulations. He's tall and built and gorgeous, and when he looks at me all I want to do is crawl into his lap."

"And have you?"

"Yes." Linn's voice was glum. "More than once." She looked up. "Stop that."

Natalie attempted to wipe the grin off her face. "I'm not laughing. This is serious. But you know what it sounds like to me?"

"An internal investigation waiting to happen?"

"No, dear heart. It sounds like maybe you've met your match. Someone you can't freeze with that look you have. Roddy Baker hasn't thawed yet, and you laid it on him a year ago."

"Roddy Baker needed it."

"If you're climbing into this guy's lap, maybe he's different. Maybe he's the one for you."

Linn moved Natalie's stapler to the right a few inches, then back to its original position. "It sounds like you've been talking to my sister."

"Your sister is a woman of discernment. So am I. Get a clue."

Linn looked up. "That's what they have on their caps. Get a CLEU."

"Stop changing the subject. So the guy is your team lead. Aside from tingles where they shouldn't be, what do you think of him?"

Linn opened her hands, palm up. "The guys have already given me the lowdown. He's a short-term guy with a preference for out-of-town operators. But I still don't know why…" Her voice trailed away.

If he preferred short-term relationships, then pursuing Caroline was understandable. But what about last night? What about the guy who knew the Latin names of flowers and liked the smell of lime-scented soap on her? She'd give a lot to know if he revealed that kind of thing to his out-of-town flings.

"Don't know what?" Natalie prompted.

"Just some things he says and does that make me wonder."

"Okay, that's him. What about you?"

"I could fall," Linn confessed finally. "Against my better judgment. Tessa says I'm running away from emotional involvement and making up excuses."

"Tessa's probably not half in love with her boss."

"I'm not half in love with him!"

Natalie grinned. "Okay, okay. You're not. Admitting you could fall is a major concession on your part, though."

"For all the good it does me. He's still my lead."

"If you're discreet, you can pull it off."

Linn narrowed her eyes at her friend. "This sounds like the voice of experience."

"It is."

The two women exchanged a long look. "You've got to be kidding me," Linn said at last. She ran through all the possibilities in her mind, her mental Rolodex flipping cards until it stopped at one. "Wait. Don't tell me. Terrance Lee?"

Nat nodded and glanced at the open door. She lowered her voice. "The very same. We'll be having our two-year anniversary shortly. And celebrating it very quietly and very far away from Santa Rita PD."

Linn felt a little winded. Terrance Lee had been her boss. The head of the detective division. He was experienced and sharp and completely by the book, or at least she'd thought so until now. But he'd always had a soft spot for Natalie, had sent work her way that would be sure to get her noticed by the brass. He'd even asked for her as the ident specialist on a suspected parental abduction that had been in all the papers, and her analysis of a partial print had helped them land the real perpetrator.

"Wow," she said slowly. "Terrance Lee."

"So you see, it can be done."

"Right, until it goes bad and I have to request a transfer."

"Linn Nichols, you need to stop looking at things in terms of when they're going to end. That's a relic from your parents being so undependable and you know it. You can't operate that way all the time in real life."

"I'm just being a realist."

"Pessimist. Not the same thing," Nat said, shaking her head.

"Listen to you. Real life is about playing by the rules. Watching where the boundaries are. Setting your own."

"So set them a little further out."

"Then what's the point of abiding by the rules?"

"Sometimes there isn't a point. Sometimes you have to find out what you want and pursue it."

"Spoken like a true anarchist. No rules. Do what you want. That's what we're here for, Nat. To rein in all the people who do exactly that."

"I'm not talking about the law. I'm talking about ourselves. Sometimes it's worth the risk if what you want is out there a little way. Sometimes you just have to step outside the boundaries and go for it."

"The way you did."

"Exactly."

"Are you guys getting married?"

Nat gave her another don't-change-the-subject look. "We've talked about it. Maybe."

"And you think I should break the rules and see

where it takes me. You are a stellar example of law enforcement ethics at their best, Natalie Wong."

"No, I'm not." She grinned at Linn. "I'm a woman in love. And believe me, the risks are worth it."

## 9

*THE RISKS ARE WORTH IT.*

Linn parked in the underground garage of the temporary house and hefted her black rolling suitcase out of the back of the SUV. Nat and Terrence Lee. Who knew?

Sure, he was pushing fifty and Natalie had just thrown a Dirty Thirties party for herself, inviting Linn and several of their closest girlfriends only a few months before. But he and Nat were both smart and intuitive, and they had the same way of looking at a case that brought success and kudos to the department. They were part of a team in a way that Linn wanted to be and wasn't with her own co-workers at CLEU.

As proven by the continued absence of the navy-blue ball cap.

And yet it was obvious Terrence satisfied Natalie in a way that a younger man couldn't. That smile of hers had held deep happiness and a sense of rightness about her choices.

Linn bumped the suitcase up the concrete stairs and tried not to envy her too much.

The door at the top opened. "Here, let me take that." Kellan hefted the heavy bag as if it weighed nothing, and she followed him inside.

She'd toured the house the week she'd signed on, and it hadn't changed. There were three bedrooms in the second-floor walk-up, two for the undercover operators and one for the surveillance equipment. One and a half baths, a living room, a kitchen. Bare-bones furniture.

Pretty typical, even if CLEU was better funded than many a State agency she could name. But the agency's money went toward overtime and flash rolls and all the innumerable things that made covert operations successful. Not furniture and carpet.

She should be grateful the walk-up had three bedrooms and not two. Or one. She'd slept with recording equipment before, and it wasn't an experience she wanted to repeat very often.

"I took the room at the back," Kellan said over his shoulder. He wheeled her bag into the other room. "Hope this is okay."

"It's fine." Two doors between them was a good thing.

He stood the suitcase up at the foot of the bed, which hadn't been made up yet. A flat stack of sheets and blankets sat on the bare mattress. The only other piece of furniture was a bureau. The closet door was folded back, and a couple of empty hangers pinged against each other as they moved in the breeze from the open window.

It was amazing how much of the eight-by-ten

space Kellan took up. He wore a red tank top that dipped low over his pecs and showed a furred chest that could make a grown woman whimper. And shorts. Black shorts that showed off thighs like iron—beautifully sculpted, rugged iron.

She, on the other hand, was still dressed in the navy pantsuit and white blouse she'd worn to court that afternoon. He was hot and sexy and virile. She was cold and businesslike and had a high white collar.

But put them in the same room together, plastered all over one another, and he would melt her soon enough. He'd unbutton the blouse and warm her skin and heat her blood to the screaming point, and the room would be full of steam as they combusted togeth—

"Are you okay?" He leaned over a little to look into her eyes. "Do I have something on my face?"

"What?" Dear God. She had to learn to control her expression, not to mention the fantasies that were happening behind it. She lifted the suitcase onto the bed and began to fiddle with the zipper. "I was just thinking about something else."

"What kind of clothes do you have in there?"

She fixed him with a glance that in no way resembled the unfocused weirdness of a moment before. "Appropriate ones."

"Like what?"

"Why are clothes so important to you? What difference does it make? I know what Caroline wears."

"If you were in court today, you didn't have time

to go shopping. And I'm betting what Caroline wears doesn't normally live in your closet."

"Don't bet on horses," she suggested calmly. "As it happens, I have a few things." The zipper screeched around its track, and she flipped open the suitcase. "White shirt, black bra." She slid her palm under each item and lifted it like a pizza on a tray. "Dress, red. Sundress, white. Jeans, tight. One pair of shorts, khaki. Two T-shirts. One tank top. One blouse, see-through." Deep breaths, through the nose. "Happy?"

"One investigator, happy. Your clothes are fine. Geez, lighten up."

She wanted to take the neatly rolled T-shirts and beat him about the ears with them. "I am not incompetent. Quit trying to make me feel as if I am. Concentrate on the big stuff, like keeping us alive this weekend."

One sable eyebrow rose, disappearing into the shaggy mane that flopped into his eye. "I make you feel incompetent?"

"This control thing you have."

"We talked about this before."

"Yes, but it didn't sink in. That's the effect that control has on people, Kellan. It makes them feel incompetent when you ride right over their choices and thoughts."

"Okay, how's this. Do you feel like ordering in something to eat? The State doesn't stock this place and I'm no cook."

"Chinese would be great."

"I was thinking more of a pizza."

She threw her hands in the air. "See, that's just what I mean! You give me a choice and take it away again. Don't bother next time and save me the grief."

He frowned a little, studying her as if she were something new and puzzling. "If you want Chinese, that's okay, too."

"Yes. I. Want. Chinese."

"Women," he muttered as he went out of the room. She could hear him hunting around for a phone book. "Always so fussy."

When the food came, it was hot and smelled wonderful. While Kellan got out his stacks of files for a working meal, Linn spooned Szechuan beef and tender bok choi simmered in garlic over the hills of steaming rice on each paper plate.

After getting her own way over the ethnicity of the food, she'd let him choose the dishes. It didn't do to overwhelm a man with too much information. Fortunately, his favorites and hers seemed to be pretty similar.

"I'm glad you like things hot," she told him over O'Reilly's open folder. "I love red chili and fresh veggies. If you were the kind of guy who thought chicken balls were Chinese food, I'd have gone and got that pizza."

"You like things hot, do you?" He pushed his empty plate away and watched her use her chopsticks to fish the very last piece of beef out of the bottom of the cardboard container.

"I have jalapeño chiles growing in pots on my

patio." She savored the crispy beef. "What's that in Latin?"

"*Capsicum* something. I don't think Mom put those in her flower arrangements. But I didn't mean hot as in spice. I meant hot as in life."

Linn swallowed the beef before she'd quite finished chewing it. "What makes you say that?" Hadn't the women closest to her just finished telling her she was too structured, too busy running away? "Never mind, I don't think I want to know."

"How are you going to get out of having sex with Rick O'Reilly, if he pushes you?"

The beef lodged in her throat, and she coughed.

"You okay?"

"I'm fine." She got up and reached for one of the four plastic cups in the cupboard, filled it with water and drained it.

When she came back to the table, she had an answer. "If it really gets to that point, and I don't think it will, I'm going to get him drunk. Or help it along with a Valium tablet or something."

He huffed a laugh. "Not gonna work."

"Why not?"

"Because Tricky Ricky never gets drunk. He may get blasted in the comfort of his own home, but he never lets his guard down in a business situation. Doesn't drink to excess, doesn't sample the product. You want to talk about control? Tricky Ricky is the ultimate guy behind the curtain, making sure everyone dances to his tune."

She sat back and mulled over the new information. "I'll think of something," she said at last. "Lord knows, I've had enough practice with you."

KELLAN GAVE HER a long, measuring look. It wasn't that he wanted to shake her self-confidence. She'd proven she could think on her feet. But some things were just too hard to resist. "Don't forget, we're sleeping together, too. Unless he's got it arranged so we don't, in which case Jealous Guy will join the party."

He'd make damn sure of that for a couple of reasons. First, of course, he couldn't put her in a situation where she'd be alone with Rick O'Reilly and in physical danger. And second, if she was going to play Caroline, he was going to play Dean to the hilt. And that meant sleeping together, eating together, doing whatever it took. Together.

"Kellan, we can't share a room. It's totally against policy for two operators to do that on the job."

Just how far did she think policy was going to get them in this situation?

"Linn, you're not in Santa Rita anymore. This is CLEU, and contrary to what's printed on the letter-head, our real motto is Whatever It Takes."

He wasn't into self-deception. This was no longer about the job. This was all his protective instincts rushing to the surface to take care of the barefoot girl in the bathrobe. Yes, she had a problem with that. Yes, she could take care of herself. But he was still going to do his level best to make sure she got through this operation.

And on the other side…what?

He'd jump off that bridge when he got to it.

"It's going to be hard enough for us to give each other security without you insisting on separate rooms," he went on. "Besides, that would totally blow our cover." Her gaze went a little unfocused, and he frowned. "Linn?"

She blinked. "You're right. I need to stay with you as much as possible, but without putting the possibility of an introduction in jeopardy. They may insist on you being alone for that."

"If they do, I'll make sure O'Reilly stays with me and doesn't go hunting for you. Not that I don't have every confidence you can handle yourself."

Linn nodded and began to clear the table. "I'm going to take some of these files to bed and study them for a while. Do you want to use the shower first?"

He grinned at her. "I'm a morning kind of guy. In all ways. You go ahead."

If she thought the killer glare would faze him, she had another think coming. "Is that the kind of thing Caroline is supposed to know?" she said.

"If she doesn't know now, she will by the time this is over."

LINN'S DEPARTMENT-ISSUED cell phone rang at 11:07 p.m., bringing her downhill slide into sleep to an abrupt halt. Only one person would be calling, though the number on the display was unfamiliar. He'd probably changed his phone again.

# Get FREE BOOKS and a FREE GIFT when you play the...

# LAS VEGAS
## GAME

*Just scratch off the gold box with a coin. Then check below to see the gifts you get!*

**YES!** I have scratched off the gold Box. Please send me my **2 FREE BOOKS** and gift for which I qualify. I understand that I am under no obligation to purchase any books as explained on the back of this card.

350 HDL DZ94                    150 HDL D2AK

| | |
|---|---|
| FIRST NAME | LAST NAME |

ADDRESS

| | |
|---|---|
| APT.# | CITY |

STATE/PROV.          ZIP/POSTAL CODE          (H-B-07/04)

She flipped on the bedside lamp and realized belatedly that they couldn't record the call as evidence. A "hot number" resided in the third bedroom, but they'd decided to keep things simple and just have Caroline use a cell phone.

"Hello?"

"Hey," Rick O'Reilly said in what he probably thought was a late-night DJ kind of voice. Low. Sexy.

*Gack.*

Kellan slid into the room wearing nothing but an ancient pair of sweats that clung to his hips and told her in no uncertain terms that he wore nothing underneath.

She reminded herself that the regulations dictating separate bedrooms were there for a reason. To wit, so that she didn't have to sleep with flawless pecs and ripped abs. They were there to keep her from crawling on top of him and finding out if the promise hidden under that soft gray cotton was for real.

"O'Reilly?" he mouthed, holding a hand near his ear with little finger and thumb extended in the shape of a phone.

She nodded and forced herself to do what she was getting paid to do, which was focusing on verbal evidence from the target, not the bold outline of her team lead's body.

"Were you asleep?"

Caroline. She was Caroline, who slept in a red silk camisole and may or may not be in bed with Kell—er, with Dean at this very moment.

As if he'd read her thoughts, Kellan stretched out on the empty side of the bed and leaned on one elbow to watch her. She held the phone away from her ear a little so he could hear both sides of the conversation.

"Not quite," she said softly to O'Reilly. "Here you are again. Are you missing me?"

"Oh, I was just thinking about the weekend. About you, and the fun we're going to have."

"Lucky me, with two men to see that I'm entertained."

"Only one man, sugar. Dean's going to have to take a hike."

"He might be difficult to persuade."

"When you look at it, you'll see which of us is the best investment in the long run."

Kellan's eyebrows tilted together in a frown, but his gaze never left her face.

"I always research my investments carefully," she said. "I want to make sure there's a good return. And I never gamble."

"Funny you should say that. I talked to Hidalgo Martinez this afternoon."

Linn glanced at Kellan. Here was a dangerous rock to navigate around. She knew the informant's handlers had briefed him carefully, but there was always the chance Hidalgo's loyalties to O'Reilly were stronger than the threat of incarceration.

"Did you? How is he?"

"I think you made another conquest last winter. I was almost jealous."

"He's a lovely man. Such a pity we won't see much of him in future."

"I'm sure he's got good legal advice. He did tell me one thing, though."

"What was that?" She held her breath.

"He told me you don't play around. That you're a straight shooter with good connections. My friend in Napa was real happy to hear that."

Linn exhaled. "I believe in healthy relationships, business and otherwise." Hidalgo had vouched for her, given her a rep. She wasn't just The Girl anymore. She was a player in an international game.

"Are you doing business on this trip?" O'Reilly's voice was even.

Kellan shifted, and his hair moved gently against his bare shoulders as he shook his head.

"No, darling," she assured the dealer. "I'm here strictly for pleasure, which is why I'm looking forward to the weekend, too."

"I'm glad to hear it. You in the mood for a little pleasure right now?"

"Why, are you going to send me a sample over the airwaves?"

"No, sweetheart. Get your mind off business. I mean a little fun. A little sexy talk. Just between the two of us."

Kellan mimed sticking his finger down his throat, and she barely managed to keep her face straight. She kicked him, but with her feet under the covers it didn't do much good.

"Actually," she said when she could be sure there

would be no trace of laughter in her voice, "Dean is here in bed with me at the moment. I would love a little verbal pleasure from the lips of a master, but I'd prefer it if we were alone."

"Did he hear you say that?" There was anticipation in O'Reilly's voice.

Linn glanced at Kellan. "Oh, yes, he heard. You bad man."

O'Reilly laughed. "You ain't seen nothing yet, sweetheart." Something that sounded like a kiss came over the line. "To be continued, then. Good night."

Kellan rolled his eyes and flopped onto his back.

"Good night, darling. Until tomorrow."

She disconnected and then turned the cell phone off.

"'The lips of a master'?" Kellan inquired of the ceiling. "Good God."

"I'd like to see you do any better. How many of your targets have offered *you* phone sex?"

"None, so far. Too bad."

"You're welcome to Rick O'Reilly. Just being on the phone with him gives me an ear infection."

He rolled to face her again, his head on the other pillow, while she sat with her back against the headboard.

"Sure you want to go through with this?"

"I can do the job."

If she pulled the covers up to her shoulders, she'd look like a prim little virgin. If she slid down, he might think she was giving him an invitation. Linn settled for crossing her arms on the blanket, acutely aware that her new red silk camisole lay cool on her naked skin.

"Besides, it's too late for you to swap me out now that he's already met me."

She wished she had her old gray T-shirt on, but police-issue PT togs were definitely out of character. Kellan Black lay on her bed looking tousled and delicious, staring at her as if he'd just realized what she had on. At least you could hide behind gray cotton. Between red silk and peekaboo lace, this camisole left her defenseless.

"Kellan."

"Hmm?" His gaze rose slowly to her eyes, innocent as a cherub. A buff, tanned cherub who was making her heart do salsa steps against her ribs.

"I think you should go back to your room."

"Do you really sleep in that?"

"Only for now. I bought it on the way here. O'Reilly's going to expect it."

"Are you going to let yourself get into a situation where he sees it?"

"No, but they may go through my things. I thought it best to stay in character."

"Right down to the skin. It suits you."

"I hope not."

"Why? Are you afraid of her? Caroline?"

"She hasn't had police training." Linn's tone was dry. "She doesn't know when to stop."

"And you do."

"Which is why I'm asking you to go back to your room."

"It seems to me that two objective investigators ought to be able to share sleeping space."

He was pushing her. Seeing how far she would go before she acted. But what would she do? Push him out the door or pull him closer?

This was impossible. Half of her wanted the first and the other half needed the second.

"I seem to remember something from the other night that makes me disagree." If she didn't look at him, maybe he would stop testing her powers of resistance. Because even as her brain was telling her she shouldn't get involved, that it was too risky to her career, her breathing was already shallow with anticipation.

"We need to get comfortable with showing our attraction, Linn." His voice dropped to a whisper. He sat up and ran a finger along her bare arm. "How are you going to pull this off if you barricade yourself behind the blankets every time I get close to you?" With the same finger, he tugged at the blanket she'd managed to work up under her arms. "In a manner of speaking."

"I'll improvise." She wished her voice sounded more authoritative, and not quite so breathless.

"Improv only works in the theater." He breathed the words in her ear.

When his lips dropped to her shoulder, then traveled to her throat, she forgot the sensible reply she should make. How could any woman think about sensible replies when Kellan Black's tongue and teeth were doing delicious, feathery things on her skin?

He kissed her shoulder and pulled the blanket down all the way. "We don't need this, do we?"

Before she could think any further, she found herself flat on her back, the pillows pushed out of the way, and her mouth opening under his.

He kissed the way an artist painted or a race-car driver drove—with fire and passion and total concentration. In a kiss like that, there was no room for sensible replies or even rational thought. There was only Kellan Black and the way he made her feel.

She wrapped her arms around his neck and welcomed his tongue, strong and hot. Kissing wasn't against regulations. They could practice kissing without getting themselves into trouble.

His mouth was amazing. Her temperature rose and her body melted, her thighs parting of their own accord under the weight of his leg. Her tongue responded to the seduction of his, advancing and retreating, circling his, sucking.

He rolled a little to the side, and she went with him. When his hand tented, hot and possessive, over her breast and its fragile layer of silk, she made a little sound of pleasure in her throat. His thumb stroked her nipple, teasing it, sending tremors of delight through her body.

"I love the way you respond," he whispered.

Responding to him came as naturally as breathing. She wanted him to look, to touch, to taste—and she wanted it now.

He must have sensed it, because he pulled the

camisole up over her head, slowly, and for the first time, she was naked from the waist up under his hot gaze. She forgot that this was her team lead. She forgot they were investigators at all. He was man and she was woman and her body was desperate to have his mouth on her, hungry for his skin against hers.

"I'll have to be careful with this, won't I?"

Her camisole was bunched in his hand, like a soft blown rose. He lowered it until the lace edge barely touched her collarbone, then moved it with excruciating slowness across her skin.

"Kellan…"

"Wait," he whispered. "We have time."

Once, in what seemed like another life, she'd wondered what it would be like to have someone make love to her with a feather. It must be something like this—the exquisite torture of wanting without being able to have, of being touched without really being touched. Oh, yes, she could grasp his wrist and tell him to stop, that she needed more, but then she'd miss out on each tickling sensation of the lace as it circled her breast and began its ascent.

*Just let him adore your body,* whispered a voice in the back of her mind. Caroline's voice. *Live the moment. Love it.*

With a sigh of pure pleasure, she relaxed, just as he drew the lace across her hardened, aching nipple, where it caught and held, as if he were making a decision whether to stop or to go on.

Breathlessly, she waited, and the fabric began to

move again, lace leading the way, the smooth coolness of the silk following—not a consolation prize, but a promise of things to come.

He teased the other breast, taking his time, sending trails of sensation over her skin each time he moved. Then he took a detour and skimmed the fabric down her ribs to her belly, still with deliberate slowness. She had never been watched this closely before, every movement of his depending on each reaction of hers. Such single-minded concentration was erotic in itself, as if all that mattered to him was the pleasure each second brought to her.

But each second was bringing her closer to that place of total, abject need, and when he brushed her thighs with the soft fabric, she didn't think she could bear a fresh assault on her senses.

"Kellan, please...I can't stand it."

"I know." His voice was husky. "I can't, either. I've been wanting you this way for days."

What way? Naked and breathless with desire?

Her fingers wrapped around his wrist and she met his gaze with wicked promise. "My turn." He had been holding the fabric loosely, and before he could react, she'd pulled the camisole from his hand.

"No fair."

"I'll show you fair."

She began as he had, at the collarbone, the lace catching and tickling as she drew it across the mat of hair on his chest. She circled his nipples, but didn't leave him the way he'd left her. Oh, no. Leaning on one elbow, she bit each one gently, teasing with her tongue. He made a muffled sound, and she smiled with satisfaction.

He must have been watching for her to get smug. "See how you like it," he growled. Rolling toward her, he lowered his mouth to her breast and sucked her deeply into his mouth. His tongue was just as skillful with her nipple as it had been earlier with her mouth, and he courted it the same way, flicking, sucking, advancing and retreating. He moved to the other nipple and pleasured her there, too, and her body took up a slow rhythm, her hips moving against him in a speechless demand.

His erection tented the front of his sweats, standing at full mast. She flattened one hand on his abdomen and slid it down to cup him through the fabric. Air hissed through his teeth as she measured his length, squeezing softly. She tugged on the drawstring, and the waistband relaxed, and in a second she'd pulled his sweats off and tossed them away.

She found the camisole where she'd dropped it, and slid the fabric across his belly, up and over his erection, to his thighs. The silk slid across his skin as though it were liquid, pooling between his legs before it slithered across his hip.

"We're going to ruin that thing before we ever get to Napa," he said tightly.

"This is what it's made for."

"Maybe. But I need more," he confessed in a whisper, and she smiled.

Some men needed clothes to make them stare-worthy. Some men were better to look at without any at all. Kellan Black was the kind of man who looked good in anything—or nothing. Linn marveled at the play of muscle as she ran a hand over his belly. At this moment she particularly liked nothing.

She took him in hand, and the breath he'd been holding whooshed out of him. Liquid beaded on the tip of his cock, and she smoothed a little of it over the plumlike head, circling it, learning the shape and textures of him.

"Linn," he croaked.

"Mmm?" She wanted to take him in her mouth. She wanted him to plunge into her body. She wanted him half a dozen different ways—it was only a matter of choosing which one.

"I need to get something out of my room."

"Now?"

"Yes, now, unless you want me coming in your hand."

She considered that for a moment. "Such a waste."

"Then you need to let me go."

When he came back, she drank in the sight of him, tanned and glorious, swollen and stiff with desire. For her. With quick movements he tore the condom package open and sheathed himself.

He piled the pillows against the headboard. "Come here, gorgeous," he suggested. "Sit in my lap."

The camisole fell under her knee as she straddled him and felt the insistent beat of his cock against her buttocks. She reached beneath her and stroked his length. He jumped, as though her touch had made a bolt of sensation rocket through his body. He cupped her mound with one hand and slid a finger into the creamy wetness that waited for him.

"You're as ready for me as I am for you."

Two fingers stretched her, stroked her. Reminded her how long it had been since a man had touched her this way. And it had been longer still—perhaps never—since anyone had touched her with such skill. He seemed to know exactly the moment when she could stand it no longer, and his wet fingers slid out of her body and over her clit.

She was so swollen, so ready, that she jumped with the little burst of pleasure. He began to stroke her, and she knew she wouldn't last more than a couple of seconds.

"I need you now."

As he explored the curves of her breasts with his tongue, he tilted his pelvis up and she impaled herself slowly, her hands on his shoulders, her head thrown back as her body opened to him.

"That's so good," she sighed, and began to move, sheathing him again and again, savoring each thrust and the way he filled her, stretched her, even. His thighs trembled and his skillful fingers again found her clit, stroking her in a counterpoint to the rise and fall of her body. The tension built with each wave of pleasure.

She couldn't stop it. She didn't want to stop it. An orgasm she couldn't control or slow down slammed through her, and fireworks blossomed behind her closed eyelids.

As she shuddered with the pleasure of it, still pumping up and down on him, he braced himself on both arms and drove up into her with a powerful flex of his hips. His body froze in a split second of stillness, and then his release hit him, making his back arch as he gripped her waist with both hands and called something—a word? a name?—into the swinging curtain of her hair.

# *10*

SHE JERKED UPWARD, and Kellan slid out of her body with a suddenness that left him cold and confused.

"What did you call me?"

He fell back on his elbows and reached out, still half-delirious with the pleasure he'd experienced with her. He wanted to feel her, warm and languorous, against him, to prolong it for just a few minutes more.

She scrambled back, and her hand fell on the red camisole. She jerked it on. "I said, what did you call me?"

What was she talking about? "Linn. Take that off and come back here."

"You did not. You cried out. You said *Carrie.*"

He had? He tried to remember, but she was crouched on the bed like an angry cat ready to spring, and he needed to do something about that, fast.

"Come here, sweetheart. Let's talk about this. People can get so deep into character that they talk about themselves in the third person. But I didn't just make love to Caroline. I made love to you. Linn Nichols."

"But when you came, you called her name, not mine."

Whether he had or he hadn't, that wasn't the point. The point was getting back to that place where they could lie next to each other. He reached for her pillow, which was teetering on the edge of the bed, and plumped it into place beside his. Now was not a good time to match her tone. Instead he kept his voice low. "Why does it bother you so much?"

Her shoulders drooped a little as the spurt of agitation began to drain away. Had she been hoping he would fight with her, to give her an excuse to leave?

"I don't know. I'm beginning to think I have a split personality."

He judged the moment might be right to take her wrist in his fingers and tug her toward the pillow. To his surprise she came.

"But I don't want to be split," she went on slowly. "I don't want this to be Dean and Caroline, just part of the job. I want this to be you and me."

This was more like it. "For me it was."

They lay side by side, facing each other, voices quiet. The way it had been the other night, in her apartment. He wanted that sense of intimacy, like a secret room in the middle of the State's temporary housing. This was what he missed when he was working. That connection with other people—normal people. People who weren't criminals. Sometimes he had to go two or three months at a time without so much as making a phone call to any of his family. He'd lost track of the birthdays and holidays he'd had to give up because there wasn't a way to break off an operation and become a civilian for a weekend.

"It's something we all deal with," he said softly. "The split personality. If I went to see my family as Dean they'd disown me, but after spending six or eight weeks living and breathing Dean, who's done hard time for distribution, it's pretty difficult to be Uncle Kellan for my nephews."

The corners of her mouth lifted in a halfhearted smile. "And Uncle Kellan can't talk about weekend house parties and spending hundreds of thousands in one day and driving fancy cars, either, can he?"

"No. Uncle Kellan's life is pretty boring in comparison. Sometimes it scares me. Life as a criminal is definitely not boring. Sometimes it can be addictive. The adrenaline. Having to think on your feet all the time. The challenge of getting the better of these guys."

"Are you addicted?"

He thought about that. "Not addicted. But sometimes disoriented. Like driving down the freeway and suddenly realizing I don't know who I'm supposed to be at that particular moment. That's pretty weird."

"Does that happen when you're with Caroline?"

"She's very disorienting." He smiled at her, then sobered. "Caroline makes it easier to be Dean."

"She's part of that fast life. Lots of money and easy women."

"We could write a country-western song."

"No, thanks. It would have to be a blues song. With Albert Collins on guitar."

Kellan grinned. "In that case we'd have to have no money and a hard woman."

To his delight, she laughed. "You're right." Then something seemed to strike her and the smile faded from her mouth. "That's me. No money to speak of. And some people see me as a hard woman."

"I don't." He meant it. Of all the faces of Linn and Caroline put together, this was the one he liked best. This was the girl in the green bathrobe. "Now that I know you better."

She was silent, her eyes focused on something inside herself. A breeze blew through the open window, and a car went by on the street outside with its stereo turned up loud enough to make the glass vibrate.

When the sound faded, he asked gently, "Can I stay?"

Her gaze came back to him, her eyes dark and shadowed in the lamplight. "I don't think this is the time or the place for you to ask me that. But I might have an answer when the case is over."

Ah. He could take a hint. He tamped the disappointment and mustered a smile, then leaned over to kiss her softly. "See you in the morning. But ask yourself this. When the case is over, do you think we have a chance?"

A CHANCE? WHAT DID HE MEAN, a chance?

Linn leaned back on the buttery leather seat of the

limousine as it purred its way north to the Napa Valley wine country. Kellan's arm lay comfortably around her shoulders, and her left hand rested on his denim-clad thigh. They looked like a pair of lovebirds on their way to an all-expenses-paid tryst, but Kellan had whispered into her ear earlier that he recognized the driver. The limo company employed O'Reilly's couriers, carrying packages of narcotics all over the city under the guise of picking up well-heeled customers.

Their conversation was restricted to small talk. Which was just fine with Linn. She needed a chance to think—as if there hadn't been lots of time for that during the long hours of the night, after he'd slipped across the hall to his own room.

Yes, she was sexually attracted to him. Yes, the feelings and antagonism and sheer desire had been building up for days and the inevitable conclusion had been terrific. But the problem was, she couldn't quite get over the feeling that, despite what he'd said to reassure her, he had been making love to Caroline instead of to her. What did it say about her when a man fantasized about someone else when he was buried deep in her body?

Kellan Black was the wrong man for her, despite the way they agreed on little things. Despite the way he could make her laugh. In one way, though, it was good they'd gotten the sex out of the way. Now she could really concentrate on this case and put on her act as Caroline without the secret fear that she'd let herself go with the fantasy and get any more involved.

If Caroline was on his mind during the moment of truth—orgasm—then it was pretty certain she was the one he really wanted. Both of them knew she was a heartless, amoral bitch, so that's exactly who he'd get.

The limo tooled through the hills and slowed for the village of Napa. The clapboard shops and houses had kept their early 1900s flavor. Maybe sometime when she wasn't working, she and Tessa or Natalie could come up here and spend a weekend tasting wine and window shopping. That wasn't much to ask, was it? To get away from the job long enough to connect with people she loved. And to get back the pieces of herself she seemed to be losing. Tessa had advised her to integrate Caroline into her personality. That was turning out to be pretty difficult when Caroline made a habit of stealing the things Linn had begun to value, such as Kellan's opinion.

They turned in at a long drive flanked by pines and scrub oak draped in mistletoe. The parasite plant sucked the life out of the trees and subsequently starved to death. How had such a thing become associated with Christmas and kissing? It was a perfect metaphor for the drug trade, though, except that when the host died or got thrown into jail, the parasites just moved on to other targets.

On that happy thought, the limo glided to a stop in front of the house. Linn studied her surroundings as she got out of the car. If this were the importer's second pied-à-terre, she'd love to see what his houses looked like in Miami and wherever else he lived.

Terra-cotta-red tiles and creamy plaster baked in the sun. Bougainvillea in shades of fuchsia, purple and red exploded from trellises in the south-facing angles of the house. Cypresses and palms provided shade, and from somewhere she heard the sound of running water, which probably cost a fortune in a state where fountains and watercourses were the first to go during summer droughts.

She doubted that anything as annoying as a drought ever affected anyone at this little mission-style rancho.

"I'll take your bags up," the driver said.

She turned and saw Rick O'Reilly in the doorway, holding open one half of a pair of heavily carved Spanish doors.

"Caroline, my love." He slid an arm around her waist and kissed her on the mouth. She was less aware of the taste of bourbon than of how big a man he was, and how dangerous. She'd received her ratings in both sharpshooting and self-defense, but she was reminded again that in a physical contest with Rick O'Reilly, no matter how strong she was, chances were good she'd lose. It wasn't a comforting thought.

In the next moment she was freed as Kellan pulled O'Reilly's arm away and shook his hand.

"Welcome." O'Reilly looked him over.

"We've been looking forward to this." Kellan's tone was just as smooth, his words just as false.

Well, it wasn't as if they were all best buds. She was determined to see O'Reilly spend his life in prison, and he probably only tolerated Kellan because he was the buyer.

"I'll show you up to your rooms and you can change or whatever." O'Reilly led them into a huge, cool hall. Plaster walls painted white contrasted with the warm reds and browns of the flagstone floor. "Drinks by the pool whenever you're ready. Down the stairs and out that door." He pointed.

"Is your friend here?" Kellan inquired. "The one who owns the winery?"

"He's coming tonight. Don't worry. I said I'd introduce you and I will."

"I wasn't worried," Kellan replied. "Did you say *rooms?*"

O'Reilly entered a long wing on the ground floor and opened a door about halfway down. "Yeah. This one's yours. Caroline, you're the next door down, on the end."

"Wait a minute." Kellan didn't waste a glance on his room. "Where are you sleeping?"

"Across from Caroline. I liked the view. Hope you don't mind I took that one."

"What I mind is separate rooms. Caroline and I are here together, and don't you forget it."

O'Reilly rolled his eyes, as if Kellan were being unbelievably unsophisticated and a pain in the ass, besides. "There's a connecting door, for God's sake. She can sleep where she wants, and if that includes the room across the hall, well—" he shrugged "—who am I to argue?"

"Don't count on it," Kellan snapped.

"Why don't we let the lady decide?"

"Yes, why don't you?" Linn stepped between them and strolled to the door of her room. "See you at the pool."

When she stepped inside, she closed the door behind her and looked around. This room, and probably all the rooms in the house, had been professionally designed. The bedspread and curtains were a biscuit-colored fabric that looked like silk but was probably a longer-wearing synthetic. Still, it picked up a matching color in the rug that lay on the flagstones. It was as if the designer wanted to keep the room fairly neutral so that the view was the main focal point.

Linn walked to the windows. On this side of the house, the hillside dropped away and then rose again where the vineyard began. Acres of vines roped across the curves of the hills, rich with foliage that concealed the young grapes. Her mother would have a field day painting here.

What a shame this beautiful place was in all probability a money-laundering operation. Turning away, she went to the adjoining door and opened it—and jumped back with a gasp.

"Relax, it's me." Kellan lowered his hand, fisted to rap on the door, and leaned in. "So, are we using your room or mine? Yours has more windows."

"But it's closer to O'Reilly."

"Right. Mine's bigger, and the bed is a king." He peered over her shoulder. "Yours looks like a queen and my feet always hang off the end."

She could not believe she was having this conversation with her team lead. They sounded like Mr. and Mrs. Middle America at the Dew Drop Inn.

"The king, then. But we need to stay focused."

He picked up her suitcase and brought it into his room. Pulling the connecting door shut behind her, she joined him.

With a glance that told her he hadn't misunderstood, he said, "Meaning no repeats of last night? You can put pillows down the middle if you want."

She ignored that and changed the subject. "This place is beautiful. It could pass for a honeymoon heaven easily, except that knowing what it really is kind of puts a damper on the romance."

"True. You don't sign into the average honeymoon heaven knowing your room will probably be rifled and at any moment another guest could pull a gun on you."

If she felt strange and uncomfortable talking about beds with him, it was nothing to how she felt about pulling her underwear out of her suitcase and putting it into the bureau drawers. Finally she concluded she was going to have to think of the room as a dormitory and of him as a roommate, both sharing accommodations while they were at the academy for some training. Otherwise, the thought of him looking at her lacy bras and watching her hang the red dress was going to spook her and get her thinking about him in a way that was dangerous to her emotional equilibrium. And a spooked woman wasn't going to be able to play this part.

Cool and focused, that was how she'd play it.

Until she realized that he was, too. In fact, he was so damn cool and focused he was unbuttoning his jeans right in front of her.

Oh, this was *so* not fair. "What are you doing?"

His fingers stilled, then undid the last button. "Getting changed."

"You could use the bathroom."

"Sweetie, let me remind you, Dean and Caroline are living together. I undress in front of you all the time."

She glanced at the doors, but they were both firmly closed. "That isn't what I meant. You said yourself we couldn't have a repeat of last night. If you strip in front of me it's going to be really hard to keep my focus."

It didn't help when he crossed the room in nothing but his boxers and bent to swipe a pair of white cotton pants out of his suitcase. The man's ass would make Michelangelo reach for his paintbrush.

He turned sooner than she expected and caught her staring. "Do I make you lose focus?"

With any other man she'd have dismissed a question like that as flirtation or arrogance. With Kellan, she realized, she could no longer think on those terms.

"You know you do."

"And that's bad?" He pulled on a tank top and caught up a loose, crinkled cotton jacket to match the pants. He looked as if he was ready to drink a mai tai and do the limbo. "Leaving last night out of it, let me say something. I've been living this role for six months. You've only been in it for something like a week. To be really convincing, you should let yourself go." His eyes crinkled in a sudden grin. "Feel free to grab my butt if that would help."

She wasn't even sure she was the same woman who had sat in that glass room a week ago. But could she stop seeing Caroline as an antagonist and somehow integrate herself and her alter ego the way Tessa had recommended? Could she just "let herself go" and see how it played out?

Kellan didn't seem to see her distraction. He was still strategizing. "In private we behave just as we do out there. We get so deep into the roles we forget about Linn and Kellan and just stay Dean and Caroline all the time. It's called continuity. Prevents slipups like not responding when O'Reilly calls your name."

"Continuity, huh?" She caught his glance and smiled at last, a wicked smile. "Okay. But don't say I didn't warn you."

KELLAN WASN'T SURE what he expected, but it sure wasn't what he got.

Linn's lashes drooped, and an expression of cool speculation filled her eyes. The smile faded and her lips became softer, fuller, and then she reached behind her back and unzipped her dress. His eyes widened as she shimmied her shoulders and the dress plummeted down her body to land on the floor. Under it she wore a lacy bra and underpants in a color his sisters would probably agree was called taupe, to match the linen dress.

Without a word—which was a good thing, because he couldn't have come up with a reply—she picked up the dress, hung it next to his leather jacket and pulled a filmy little white thing off the hanger.

Was she going to—

Yep, she was.

Turning her back to him, she released the catch on the bra and stepped out of her panties.

Kellan's breath stopped in his lungs. The afternoon sun highlighted one side of her body, giving her skin a creamy glow. It illuminated one half of a derriere shaped like a peach, and smooth thighs that he already knew could grip a man and bring him to orgasm.

He should have thought of this twenty-four/seven tactic days ago. He hadn't thought the effect of lamplight on red silk could be improved on, but the view here was about to make him change his mind. Before he could do much more than appreciate the toned curves that hid a police officer's strength, though, she'd slid the white thing over her head and it materialized into a curve-hugging dress that looked breezy and cool.

She turned and raised an eyebrow in his direction.

He commanded his mouth to work. "Are you—are you gonna put underwear on?" he croaked. Please God, don't let her go out there with nothing on under that dress. No bra was one thing. But no underwear within a mile of Rick O'Reilly could mean serious trouble.

"Oh, if I must." She crossed to the dresser and shimmied into a scrap of pale pink lace, then smoothed the dress down. "Come along, darling," she said in Caroline's husky British purr. She picked her sunglasses off the dresser and strolled out the door barefoot.

He caught up to her halfway down the tiled hallway and took her hand for appearance's sake.

No bra. The barest minimum of underwear. She didn't need a cover team. She needed full-body armor.

They found the pool without difficulty and stepped out of the cool darkness of the house into the brilliant late-afternoon sun.

A number of people lounged in deck chairs and splashed in the water, looking for all the world like a friendly neighborhood get-together. O'Reilly, wearing a Speedo so brief he might as well have just put on a G-string, waved them over. "What can I get you to drink?"

"Beer for me," Kellan said.

"Ice water with a lime twist, thank you, darling."

O'Reilly glanced at her. "Ice water?"

"I'm very particular about what I put in my body." Her smile was like melted chocolate, and O'Reilly fell right into it.

"I can give you a suggestion or two." He went to an outdoor bar and poured her water, perching a lime quarter on the rim of the glass.

His attention on Linn was so profound that he would have dropped Kellan's beer bottle into space whether there was a hand there to grab it or not. Fortunately, Kellan's reflexes were good, and he caught the microbrew and tipped it to his lips with a sigh of pleasure.

"All in good time, Richard."

"You're the only one who calls me that."

Kellan watched him from under his lashes. The guy's eyes were all over her. Looking for signs of underwear, no doubt. Creep.

"If you'd rather I called you what everyone else does, I will."

"No. It's fine. Come on. Let me introduce you around."

Most of their companions, it turned out, were people Kellan had met in O'Reilly's organization. No surprise. The guy with the skin that looked as if it hadn't seen the sun in his entire life turned out to be James Farley, the money guy. He had worked for a big Silicon Valley computer company before he'd seen the profit margins in the laundry business for Rick O'Reilly.

Kellan made a note to himself to have a long conversation with the financier.

"What a beautiful view." With a sigh Linn settled into a lounge chair in the shade of a huge umbrella. "I'm so lucky in my friends. Almost without exception, they have lovely houses."

"They would have to, to make a good setting for you." O'Reilly picked up her hand, turned it over and kissed her palm. Kellan could swear he saw the guy apply a little tongue, too.

Linn—Caroline, he had to think of her as Caroline—slipped her hand from his and cupped his face in a movement so smooth that even he couldn't tell if it was an evasive maneuver or not.

"Do tell me your friend's name," she coaxed. "Perhaps we've met before."

"It's Arroyo," O'Reilly said. "From Colombia via Miami and L.A. They call him 'El Peligroso.'"

Kellan froze, and his plans for cornering the financier went straight out of his head. Holy shit. El Peligroso?

She smiled. "The Dangerous One? And is he?"

"Oh, yeah." The flatness in O'Reilly's tone told Kellan he meant it. "Heard of him?"

"Only indirectly, through dear Hidalgo. I've never met him in the flesh, although his reputation as a businessman is quite extensive."

And as a murderer, political conspirator, cartel boss and all-around bad guy, his rep wasn't all that shabby, either. Every narcotics investigator in CLEU had heard about El Peligroso in one of those contexts. Kellan tried to lounge in the chair as if the sun were making him sleepy, when all the time he was trying to figure out how to get the information to headquarters in San Francisco.

This was huge. This would make his career. All their careers. Taking down El Peligroso was the kind of thing that got a cop a medal.

If it didn't get him killed first.

# 11

"EL PELIGROSO," LINN MOANED. She closed the door, locked it and sank onto Kellan's king-size bed. "Dear God."

"Getting cold feet?" Kellan tossed his cotton jacket at the back of a chair and leaned a shoulder on the wall, watching her. "If you are, tell me now. You can fake an allergy to something at dinner and we can have you out of here in half an hour."

"I am not quitting!" She jumped to her feet and walked to the window. The view of the rolling, vine-covered hills should have been comforting, but it wasn't. It just reminded her how isolated they were in the face of this new danger. "Even you have to admit this is huge."

"Yeah, I know. But if you keep your cool we can pull it off."

"My cool? Who says I'm losing it?"

"You're losing your accent." His tone was dry. "Remember, we stay in character all the time."

"Oh, bugger you!" she exclaimed.

"Much better. So, how are we going to let head-quarters know about this?"

"Uh, call them?"

"Uh-huh. And you think O'Reilly isn't monitoring communications?"

She hadn't thought about that. "If he's that good, he's probably monitoring what we're saying, too."

"I don't think so. I couldn't find anything. I wouldn't be talking this freely if I had."

She hadn't thought about listening devices, either. She was too green for this. She'd gone from busting street-level distributors straight to El Peligroso, and her ears were still popping from the ascent.

And that was the least of it. Her biggest problem was standing right in front of her. Every movement, every word took her mind off doing the job and put her awareness squarely on him, and she couldn't afford to think that way right now.

"We're going to have to improvise," she said aloud, struggling to focus. "Arroyo won't come alone. At his level, I'd say four bodyguards were a minimum. But I doubt they're prepared to do a deal here and now. So we won't need to arrange a takedown on short notice, off our own turf."

"I'd say you're right. So the plan of action is to socialize, gain trust and pick up whatever we can. Keep your ears open."

Dinner was at eight, and when they all sat down together, Linn found herself on Rick O'Reilly's left at the head of the table.

"Does this winery actually produce, or is it merely a real estate investment for Mr. Arroyo?" she asked, scanning the bottles on the table.

O'Reilly turned the labels toward her one by one. "Oh, it produces. He has a vintner and a professional staff. The offices and production facilities are elsewhere on the property."

"That one looks lovely. What is it?"

"A 2000 chardonnay."

"Brilliant." She held her glass while he poured it, and took a sip. El Peligroso was as good at wine making as he was at importing Colombian cocaine. A man of parts.

"Too bad I have to leave after dinner." O'Reilly watched her. "Business. We could have spent a little more time together."

"And here I thought you were a man who kept his promises. All of them."

He caught her finger and sucked it into his mouth. His tongue ran up and down its length while his gaze never left her face. Then he released it with a wet pop. "Unavoidable," he said. "Maybe I'll call. That is, if Dean doesn't mind."

"I don't care whether he minds or not. But…" She paused and glanced down the table, then returned her gaze to his. "I'm not sure I'd like my calls from you to be monitored."

"I wouldn't call on the house phone."

"Cell phones are safe?"

"Much to my boss's annoyance."

"How lovely. I'll look forward to that, then."

Linn wondered if the "business" would take him away before the introduction was made, or if it was connected. But it wasn't likely O'Reilly would tell her. She gazed around the dining room at the heavy drapes and Victorian furniture, at the real china at each setting. Did the staff know whom they were working for? And if so, did their paychecks come out of the drug money or the vineyard?

Probably the latter. A smart businessman—and Arroyo was nothing if not smart, running his organization with the calm efficiency of a board chairman—he would want all the external elements to be legal. He probably even paid U.S. taxes.

Whatever he paid the person who prepared their dinner, it wasn't enough, she decided, returning to her plate. The lamb was succulent and the salads little works of art.

If she'd been focused less on trying to pick up tidbits of information, such as the phone situation, she might have enjoyed the food more. But with Kellan on her other side, she was kept busy trying to keep him and Rick O'Reilly from killing each other until the dessert course came.

As the pears in wine sauce were served, there was a commotion near the door and four men walked into the dining room. Three of them were built like linebackers and were dressed in black linen suits. The fourth man was tall and swarthy, wearing a suit cut so beautifully it screamed *handmade in Milan*.

*El Peligroso.* The surveillance photos didn't do him justice.

"Enrique." O'Reilly rose to greet him. "Have you eaten yet?"

Arroyo nodded. "Yes, on the plane. Who do we have here?"

While the bodyguards stood at attention near the door, O'Reilly introduced everyone in turn. "And this is Dean Wilcox, who I told you about, and his lovely lady, Caroline…?" He paused and Linn suddenly remembered she had never been introduced with a surname.

"Pennington," she said. "From London. *Soy feliz de encontrario,* Señor Arroyo."

"And I to meet you." He bent to kiss her on both cheeks. "How well you speak Spanish."

"Hidalgo taught me a little last year," she said, "so that I wouldn't be utterly cheated in the markets. I have a dreadful weakness for straw hats and painted parrots."

"I am rather fond of Oaxacan art, myself." He smiled, his teeth even and white, his manner full of Old-World charm. "I'll be sure to send you one of my favorite artist's pieces the next time I'm there."

"How kind you are." He was. It was like flirting with someone's really sexy, good-looking grandfather.

"And now, Mr. O'Reilly, I believe we had a meeting scheduled."

"We did. Later, all." O'Reilly's glance took in the whole room and ended with Linn, when it took on a special significance. "Much later, hmm?" His voice was for her ears alone, but she saw Kellan's shoulders stiffen.

Throughout the rest of the interminable evening,

Kellan pretended to get progressively more drunk, until finally she led him back to their room. Once the door was shut behind them, he straightened and stretched.

"Nice job," Linn told him. "I bet even Rigby's girlfriend changed her mind about sleeping with you."

"Rigby's girlfriend has been sampling the product. I doubt she's in very good shape for anything right now."

"I've got good news."

"What's that? Way to make points with Arroyo, by the way. You don't really collect painted parrots, do you?"

A blush thought about sneaking onto her face, but she fought it back. "Yes, I do. I've only been to Mexico once, but I got a parrot and a chicken. They're hanging in my condo."

"I didn't see them."

"In the bedroom." A little silence fell, and across it, Linn felt a tingle of awareness, as though electricity had arced across the space between them. *No. This can't happen. Not here, when we're in so much danger of discovery.* "So, do you want to know about parrots or about what I found out?" Better to get the conversation back on track.

"What did you find out?" He didn't sound as if he really wanted to know.

For once in her life, Linn wished she had Tessa's sensitivity to what people were thinking. "They're not monitoring our cell phones."

"Of course they are."

She overlooked the contradiction and stayed on course. "O'Reilly wants to call later, so I asked him if the cell phones were monitored. He said they weren't."

"And you believed him."

"Well, I certainly don't want anything from him recorded. The less I have to remember him by, the better."

"That's a piece of luck if it's true." Kellan pulled off his shoes and began to unbutton his collarless white linen shirt. Her eyes followed his fingers as they made their way carelessly down the row of buttons. He shrugged it off and hung it up, giving her a nice view of his back. Muscles contracted and flexed in the simple task of hanging up the shirt.

It wasn't fair. No matter what angle you viewed the man from, he was delicious. Toned, tanned and not an extra ounce of fat on him.

"So what did O'Reilly mean by 'later'?" he asked.

"I guess he means he's going to call."

"At least you don't have to figure out how to not sleep with him."

This wasn't Jealous Guy. This was Kellan, who was honestly concerned. And who had the kind of shoulders made for bearing responsibility and crying on, if a woman were so inclined. Whose chest was a wall of hard muscle, and who could stop a woman's heart simply by standing there in nothing but his trousers.

What had he said? Oh, O'Reilly. "A call I can handle. But from a woman's point of view, he is one scary guy up close and personal."

He smiled, a slow smile that said Danger Ahead. "What does the woman's point of view say about me?"

"I think Rigby's girlfriend made that pretty clear. She was draped all over you like a feather boa."

"I'm more interested in what you think."

Could she say it? What would he think if she revealed how she really felt? Turning away, Linn toed out of her sandals and reached behind to undo the clasp at the waist of the red dress. But the two tiny hooks had tangled in the thread loops, and she couldn't get them loose.

"Want a hand with that?"

Before she could answer, he'd crossed the room and moved her fingers aside. The heat from his body radiated onto the skin revealed by the dress's plunging back, and her breath caught. When he moved the hooks aside and she felt the waistband loosen, goose bumps tiptoed from waist to shoulder.

"I know you're not cold," he whispered behind her. "It's seventy-five degrees outside. And I'm still waiting for your point of view."

"You know how I feel," she whispered back, half to him and half to the closet door.

"I want to hear it."

She'd resolved to let Caroline in, hadn't she? The old Linn would insist on at least the metaphorical equivalent of pillows down the middle of the bed. She would insist on both of them sharing quarters and being professional. But the new Linn, the one with Caroline seeping around the edges and softening her, felt Kellan's fingers slide from her spine to her ribs and let the warm touch melt her.

Her head fell back as he rested his chin on her shoulder. "I can't resist you," she confessed. "I should, but I can't."

"Who says you should?" He slipped the dress off her shoulders. "This is a no-regulations zone. O'Reilly's gone. Arroyo's in the other wing. And work is a long way away. There's no one here but us."

The red silk whispered down her legs and she stepped out of it, allowing Kellan to drape it over the closet door. When she turned to him, she was naked except for her panties and sandals. Her gaze traveled up his trousers and paused on the ridge of his erection under the fine wool.

"This isn't fair. You have more clothes on than I do."

With a sudden movement he scooped her up in both arms. "Didn't they tell you? All's fair in love in the war zone."

He laid her on the bed and, sitting beside her, took one of her feet in both hands. Gently he undid the narrow leather straps of first one sandal and then the other, taking time to caress the sensitive skin at the arch of her foot. The shoes dropped to the floor unnoticed as he slid his hands up the smooth, tanned skin of her leg.

But Linn wasn't the kind of woman who could lie passively while a man made love to her. She needed to participate. And right now what she needed most of all was to touch him. The comforter puffed around her hands as she rocked onto her knees and crawled over to where he sat. Her breasts brushed his naked back and she heard him draw in a breath. "You still have too many clothes on," she reminded him softly.

In seconds he'd taken care of that little problem. Half lifting her, half pushing her onto her back, he carried them both the length of the bed and lay with his head cradled on his bent arm, his gaze full of heat.

"Your turn." He hooked her panties with one finger and she lifted up enough for him to pull them off, taking his time on the journey down the length of her legs. With a flick, they landed on the bureau. He lay down beside her. "Now we're even."

The late-night stubble felt rough under her finger as she trailed it along his jaw and touched his mouth. In greeting, he moistened it with his tongue. "I suppose everyone tells you how beautiful you are," she said.

"That's what I was going to say."

Her hair moved on the pillow as she shook her head. "It's true. When I saw you on the other side of the glass that first day I couldn't take my eyes off you. Couldn't concentrate. You were like a silent explosion, and I've been trying to find all the pieces ever since."

"Maybe you need new pieces." With a hand flat on her belly, he traced the outline of her hipbone with his fingers. "Or some help to look."

"Maybe." She was finding it more and more difficult to remember how to string words together. The feathery touch of his hand traveled up her ribs until finally he cupped a breast. He changed position and touched her skin with his tongue. A sound escaped her throat and it seemed to spur him on to taste her, and the swirling sensation of his tongue on her breast was glorious. Nipping and sucking, he tasted every sensitive cell until it was all she could do not to beg him to move lower, to ease the ache he had created low in her belly and between her legs.

She reached for him to share some of the pleasure he was giving her. As her hands closed around his swollen length, he gasped. "Linn, if you do that I'll—"

And like an alarm telling her that she'd gone too far, the cell phone on the bureau rang.

"Oh, my God," Kellan groaned. "Somehow they always know."

"It's O'Reilly. Has to be. I can't just let it ring."

He fell back on the pillow, one arm across his eyes, and she lunged for the wretched phone. If she could have pitched it out the window she would have.

Instead she sat on the edge of the bed and resigned herself to losing the moment. "Hello?"

"Hey, baby," O'Reilly said in his late-night DJ voice. "Miss me?"

*I swear, I'm going to* so *enjoy putting you in the slammer.* "Unbearably."

"I didn't think you'd be awake."

"We've just gone to bed."

"Dean, too?"

"Of course, Dean, too."

At the sound of his alter ego's name, Kellan sat up. His gaze heated as it traced a line from the phone to her shoulder. Then he moved in on her and dropped a kiss on her shoulder blade.

She shot him a "don't you dare" look, and he grinned.

"Has your errand been a success?" She hardly knew what she was saying. Kellan moved her hair aside and his lips began to travel along the back of her neck with excruciating care. Goose bumps trailed his light kisses like the tail of a comet.

"Sure has," O'Reilly replied. "Enrique wants to have a conversation with Dean. He seemed to like you."

"I hardly spoke to him." Kellan had reached her ear now, and she shivered, trying to pull away. It was impossible to keep a conversation going when he was doing everything in his power to distract her.

And it was working.

"He has an eye for a pretty woman," O'Reilly said. "And he trusts my opinion about Dean. Much as I can't stand the guy personally because he has something I want, he's a good investment. And I know how you feel about those."

Was he going to stay on the line all night? She had what she needed—the assurance that Arroyo was going to do business with them. She had to get rid of him before she gave herself away by moaning.

Kellan slid off the bed altogether and knelt in front of her. Then he leaned in and took her nipple into his mouth. His tongue was so skilled, his lips persuading the sensitive nerve endings to utter pleasure.

Linn's whole body shuddered. "Richard, I'm exhausted. I really must say good night."

"I had planned a nightcap of phone sex with you, but you're right. I'm in the car on the Golden Gate right now and I don't want to cause an accident." He laughed.

Kellan nibbled on the inner curve of her breast.

"Good night, darling," she rasped. "I'll see you at breakfast." Then she stabbed the off button and tossed the phone aside.

"You!" was all she could manage to say before he lunged at her and they fell back on the bed together.

"Yes, me," he said. "Right here, right now and all the time."

This time she took the lead in dishing out the most pleasurable punishment she could. Rolling on top of him, she promised, "I'll show you," and kissed him. It was a full-body kiss, the kind that needed lips, chests and legs. The kind that was a direct prelude to—

"Kellan," she gasped.

"Mmm?" He nuzzled her throat, his body seeking entry to hers.

"Protection?"

He froze. After a second that seemed suspended, drawn out in midair, they looked at each other. "God."

"You didn't bring anything?" She should have.

She should have known something like this would happen. That they couldn't be trusted anywhere alone together.

"No. We're working. I didn't expect—"

Something small and joyful beat its way around her heart. He hadn't expected to make love to her. He'd planned to do the right thing, to treat her as an equal and not let the operation be sidetracked by sex. Much as they both wanted that sidetrack now.

Man, did she want it.

"I'm sorry." He rolled onto his back. "That was close. The scary thing is, I didn't even think about it."

A wicked smile began at the corners of her mouth. Stroking the line of hair on his belly that pointed the way south, she said, "I'll take that as a compliment. But meantime…"

His eyes widened as he got her drift. "God— Linn—I didn't mean—"

"Let's see if we can find a way around it." She felt raw, powerful, wicked. As un-Linn-like as it was possible to be. She lowered her mouth to his belly and rubbed her cheek on the hot skin covering the sheets of muscle. Despite his obvious strength, he seemed content to let her take the lead for once, and she took shameless advantage of it.

His skin tasted faintly of salt, a flavor that became stronger the closer she got to his erect cock. Her leisurely journey took a brief holiday on the sensitive skin where his thigh met his torso.

"Linn." The word came out through clenched teeth, and she smiled.

"This will teach you not to distract me during phone calls."

"I promise I'll never do it again. Just—"

His cock batted her cheek as she changed direction, begging for her attention. When she finally relented and took him in her mouth, he sucked air in through his teeth. She stroked him with her tongue, as if he were candy and she had all day to make him dissolve.

Out of the corner of her eye, she saw his fingers curl into the sheet, turn over and twist the fabric in his fist.

Gently, she took his testicles in one hand and massaged them, feeling how engorged they were in their sac. With her lips, she drew him up and then plunged down on him as she would have done if they had both thought to bring protection.

Through fingers and lips, she felt the tension building in him, then the moment when he relinquished all control and allowed her to pace the responses of his body.

It was like a gift, the most intimate she had ever received.

She could have drawn it out, could have made it slow and torturous, but that was for another time and place. A place that belonged to them. For now, in this hostile environment, she could give him what he needed.

She increased the pace, moving on him with suction and with her tongue. She felt the orgasm coming as he did, felt the veins flush with their burden of fluid, and with a muffled cry, he exploded into her mouth.

# 12

LINN CRAWLED UP Kellan's body to pillow her head on his shoulder while she caught her breath. His chest heaving, he rolled to meet her and wrapped his arms around her, cradling her against him.

Several minutes passed while their breathing slowed and the world stopped spinning around the core that was the two of them on the bed.

"I should forget protection more often," he murmured at last, into her hair.

"You'd better not." She kissed his jaw, tasting the fresh salt of sweat. "Wouldn't want to slow us down."

"I don't think anything will slow you down. That was amazing. Fearless. Just like you."

Fearless? Where he was concerned, that was the last word she would have used.

"Do I have something to be afraid of when I'm with you?" His chest was so warm, his arms so strong. His legs trapped hers with their weight. It had been a very long time since she'd been held like this, and she'd never felt this sense of safety. Rather than smothering her, his closeness protected.

"That depends." He loosened his hold and nuzzled

her throat. Her body, which had found some on-hold state of high arousal, kicked into gear with a jolt.

"On what?"

Lazily, he moved on to her breasts, tasting his way around each curve, and she began to lose the thread of words. "On you. On how you feel."

He reached her nipple and bit it gently, then laved it with his tongue as if to make up for the tiny violence.

"I feel your tongue. Your mouth. That's so good."

"That'll do for a start." He suckled her for long pleasurable minutes, his mouth hot on her skin, his hands gentle. He traced her ribs, one by one, and discovered the dip at her belly button. Her toes curled, her knees rising to meet him.

"Kellan, please."

"In good time," he murmured. "Your skin is so soft."

Each muscle responded to his slow kisses down the length of her thigh, and when he licked the skin at the back of her knees, she shivered. Now she knew how he felt, and the urgency built deep inside, where she had been soft and damp and waiting for what seemed like hours.

Slow kisses made the return journey up her other leg, making the tendons behind her knees tighten with anticipation. When he finally arrived at the apex of her thighs she was ready to scream.

"Ready for me?"

A strangled moan was all she could manage in reply.

At last, after an eternity of anticipation, she felt

the roughness of his cheek stubble on her inner thighs.

*Fearless,* she thought. *He's the one who's fearless. Not me.*

Her muscles loosened and she parted her legs, giving him complete access and complete control in her turn. When his tongue touched her vulva, she jerked and her fingers tangled in his hair.

"Okay?" He lifted his head.

"Please—"

He seemed satisfied at incoherence for an answer. His tongue flicked out and stroked her, once, twice, learning her shape. Then he found her clit, and Linn learned what it meant to be completely unable to gain control—and not even want it. Because there was nothing quite like Kellan's tongue making love to her, bringing her on, holding her back, intensifying the pleasure with each movement.

Without breaking his concentration on her clit, he slid a long finger into her vagina and stroked her from within.

A fireball seemed to explode behind her eyes and her orgasm exploded under his tongue, beating outward to the rhythm of his fingers. Flakes of light and sensation seemed to flash along her veins, right out to her fingers and toes, and flying out into the dark.

And this time she wanted him there to hold her when she came back down.

KELLAN WOKE SLOWLY, feeling warm and snug and boneless, despite the cool gray fog obscuring the view of the vineyard and slipping misty fingers into the open window.

He couldn't move his arm, but it didn't seem to matter. Lazily he rolled his head on the pillow and saw that Linn's dark hair was spread on his shoulder, her cheek buried somewhere between it and the pillow.

What a night. She had played him like an instrument until finally he'd had to turn his face into the pillow so the whole winery wouldn't hear him shout.

His body tightened and swelled at the memory. They had to get out of here and explore these possibilities further. She had not asked him to leave or spend the night on his own side of the bed, either. In fact, she'd grabbed him when he'd tried to give her a bit of space, and had promptly fallen asleep on his arm. As far as he was concerned, that was real progress.

The lock snicked and the bedroom door swung open. O'Reilly stuck his head in.

"Hey," he said. "Rise and shine. How's the hangover?"

Kellan's arm tightened protectively around Linn's naked body. Good thing the fog had moved in during the night to drop the temperature and make them pull the covers up. She shifted and murmured something into his shoulder.

"Get the hell out of here," Kellan snarled, trying to look as though a killer hangover were giving him a bad temper. The snarl was real enough. He could swear Linn had locked the door.

O'Reilly grinned at him. "Arroyo wants to have breakfast with you. I wouldn't keep him waiting. Sleep well?"

Beside him, Linn's legs jerked as she woke up completely and realized what was going on.

"I had one beer too many, I guess."

The grin got cockier, if that were possible. "Gotta watch that tendency. Who knows what you might miss out on."

"What are you saying?"

The dealer shrugged. "Ask your lady." His gaze moved from Kellan to the woman beside him. "Good morning, sweetheart."

"Ask her what?" He gave her a warning squeeze.

"What she does when the lights are out."

There was nothing quite so pitiful as a guy who thought he was playing mind games. Too bad Kellan had to act as though he believed him.

"Screw you, O'Reilly. Now get out of my face so I can get dressed."

Laughing, O'Reilly shut the door, and Kellan shot the bolt home. Then he came back to the tumbled bed and bent over Linn. She was still gazing at the door, as if she were afraid O'Reilly was going to come back in as soon as she threw the covers back.

"Didn't you lock the door last night?" he asked.

"Yes."

"I guess I should have expected something like it. We're lucky there was a lock at all." He frowned at the door, then glanced back at her. "Time to go to work. Arroyo wants to have breakfast with us."

She drew in a sharp breath through her nose and threw the covers back. The phone, which must have been buried in the comforter since she'd tossed it away last night, flew up and landed on the carpet. He picked it up.

"I wish I'd known he had a master key. I'd have blocked the door somehow."

"Talk about rude awakenings," Linn said. "I wonder if he's going to spend the rest of the day making up for lost time."

"What, because he saw me as winning you for the night after he got called away?"

"Something like that."

"I hope not. I hope Arroyo's being here keeps his mind on business." Kellan caught her hand. "Hey. I got ripped off."

"What do you mean?"

"I mean I wanted to wake up slowly. Maybe make love again. Probably not a good idea now, though."

He pulled her up against him and kissed her. She kissed him back, her body soft and pliant under his hands, but something was missing. Some heat or concentration that had been there last night had vanished this morning.

She pulled away a little. "If Tricky Ricky can walk in on us at will, I think I'd rather save this for a safer place."

He nodded. "Does that mean that once we get out of here, we can see each other?"

"Let's take one thing at a time."

It looked as if he was going to have to be happy with that, because she slipped out of his arms and went into the bathroom. "I'm going to take a shower."

Ten minutes later she came out, dried off briskly and pulled on another set of lacy underwear.

"Did you buy out Victoria's Secret?"

"What?"

He gestured at her bra. "So far I've seen pink, taupe and now green. I never would have expected that of you, Investigator."

He meant to tease, but she didn't take it that way. "Kellan, don't."

What? "I was giving you a compliment."

"But it's a sign of what could happen. Comments, innocent or not. Innuendo. Speculation. And heaven only knows what will happen once it gets out that we slept together."

"Who's going to tell? Not me."

"Do you think Rick O'Reilly isn't going to refer to this when he calls the hot number?"

"What's he going to say? He saw us in bed together. The whole team knows we have to play the part to be convincing. And I'll swear on a stack of Bibles that I never touched you beyond what was necessary to gain his confidence."

"You would?"

"If you want me to. I told you before, this isn't the SRPD. Things are different."

"Is sleeping with your operators different?"

He saw the trap yawning in front of his feet moments too late. "Who have you been talking to?" he asked slowly.

"It seems to be common knowledge." She wouldn't look at him. Instead she concentrated on wiggling into a short skirt.

"Why is it coming up now? You didn't ask me about other people last night."

She began to apply her makeup. "Last night was fabulous. It was like falling into a dream and not waking up. But Rick O'Reilly and this whole operation…" She gestured with a mascara wand. "This is reality. I have to stay grounded. Alert. Otherwise I'll be my own worst enemy, and we have enough of those around here already."

She was slipping away. After all that they'd done and said and felt together, she was slipping away, and doing it on purpose. "Linn, what we have now is different from my relationships with other people."

"I'm glad you feel that way."

"It isn't a dream." He was starting to feel a little desperate. She still wouldn't look at him. "This is as real as it gets. You and me, alone."

"But we aren't alone. Dean and Caroline are alone. Let's talk about reality when we can be Linn and Kellan."

"Last night we *were* Linn and Kellan." He didn't understand where she was coming from. To him, it was crystal clear. They'd created an island of reality in an environment that was based on deceit and drugs and death. A place that had been like an escape from ugliness. They'd created it together, a place that would have been impossible to create if either one was alone. And he wanted to be back in that place worse than anything he could remember wanting in a long time.

When she spoke again, the accent was back. "Come on, darling." She pulled on an embroidered camisole that brought out the color in her eyes and the creamy tints in her skin. "Let's get back on the job, shall we?"

LINN WALKED down the staircase beside Kellan, wondering how long she could keep up the front. The truth was, she didn't want to act anymore. In any other investigation, she would meet the target, set him up, take him down. But there was nothing in the training manual that told you what to do when you started to fall for your partner.

Making love with Kellan had forever changed what she was willing to settle for. Had raised the bar in what she wanted from a man. But why did it have to happen here, when there was no time to savor it, no safe place to talk about it, no opportunity to work it into their lives?

*That's just an excuse,* said something in the back of her mind. *You're using bad timing as an excuse to push him away. Again. The way you always do.*

What was the matter with her? She was a competent, respected investigator, and yet deep inside she was still a little girl, calling in the night for parents who didn't come. Natalie had been only partly right. It wasn't that her parents had been undependable. They'd reached out and grabbed life, which meant they traveled, and though she and Tessa had been cared for during their parents' absences, it wasn't the same. The end result was that she didn't expect people to stay, so they lived down to her expectations.

Kellan, it appeared, wanted to stay. Could she do something about it before he changed his mind and decided that he'd been wrong and she really was another of his short-term girls?

They reached the bottom of the staircase and crossed the flagstone hall to the dining room door. Kellan paused for a second and squeezed her hand.

That was so like him. He was supposed to be preparing himself for a mental duel with El Peligroso, and instead he gave her moral support.

*You'd better not let this one get away.*

She squeezed back, and he pushed open the door. Slanting columns of brilliant light poured in the long windows. Arroyo sat at the head of the table, buttering toast. He looked up and waved them in.

"Do you eat breakfast? I always do."

With a murmur of thanks, Linn slid into the chair he indicated on his left, and Kellan took the one on his right. Two bodyguards, she noticed, were stationed at either end of the sideboard. Rick O'Reilly took the fourth chair at the end of the table.

Arroyo handed her a bowl of fruit salad, and she spooned glistening melon balls, apricot halves and green grapes into a glass dish.

"Coffee? Hot milk?"

"*Gracias, señor.*" He pushed a carafe over to her and she poured a cup.

This was so civilized. Like being on the set of some period movie, with all kinds of double-dealing and wickedness happening all around but never mentioned in polite conversation at the table.

"Caroline. Sleep well?" O'Reilly said with a smirk.

"Never better." She smiled back at him, a smile full of sin and promise.

"Good dreams?"

"It was the strangest thing." Tasting a bit of apricot, she found it had been sweetened with some kind of lime glaze, and she sighed with pleasure. "I dreamed of having sex with you, but there was a large kitchen knife involved somehow. One of those big ones that you use to cut up beef." She paused to spear a grape. "Heaven knows what *that* means." She bit the grape in half with a neat snick of her teeth.

O'Reilly stared at her, and she could swear his skin lost color. Arroyo gave a shout of laughter. "Let's hope it doesn't mean he's cutting your product."

Kellan joined in the laughter, but O'Reilly remained distinctly subdued throughout breakfast.

Finally Arroyo turned to Kellan, and Linn sat back with her coffee. Here it came. Either they were going to be able to deal with the importer, or they would have to return to the office empty-handed and have to settle for taking down O'Reilly while Arroyo flew back to Colombia in his private plane, forever out of

reach. In any case, Kellan would be doing the nego-
tiating. Drug lords appreciated women, but they
didn't do deals with them. Linn had long ago learned
to accept it. She was here to create a convincing
background for Kellan with the reputation that had
been manufactured for her. For her to attempt anything else would irritate them at best, and at worst,
make them suspicious.

"So," Arroyo began. "I understand you are interested in a business relationship."

"I am," Kellan replied.

"There is a small difficulty. I already have a very
capable manager looking after distribution. I would
hate to create competition for him."

Kellan, with his organization charts and relationship matrix, was ready for him. "I know. I owe Rick
a lot for the introduction, and I have no intention of
cutting him out of the Bay Area market. But you have
a hole, and I think I can fill it."

Arroyo eyed him. "A hole?"

"You have California covered, but there's a good
market in Oregon and possibly even Idaho. I have
connections in those states that would make it worth
your while, considering the size of my orders."

"Oregon. Idaho." Arroyo sipped his coffee. "And
how big would those orders be?"

"Five hundred kilos, to start."

Arroyo didn't even blink, although Linn had to take
a sip of the mimosa that sat next to her place setting.
Five hundred kilos was more than Dougie Vetten
pushed through his distribution channels in five years.

"Five hundred." Arroyo appeared to think this over. "Logistically this is difficult."

"Not for you. I understand you have considerable resources at your disposal."

Arroyo inclined his head. "The wine business has its advantages."

"Oh?"

But Arroyo declined to elaborate. He was using the vineyard somehow to get the cocaine into the country. They had to find out how without sounding as though they were too interested.

"How long will it take you to collect the money?" Arroyo asked.

"Depends," Kellan said. "With that kind of volume, what kind of money are we talking?"

"Fifteen thousand a kilo, fresh off the boat," O'Reilly put in. "So two and a half million."

"That'll take me a week or so." If he was staggered at the amount of cash, he gave no sign of it. Instead, he helped himself to more coffee. "Where will we do the transaction?"

"Here," O'Reilly replied.

Now things were going to get tricky. Linn concentrated on her fruit salad and resisted the urge to catch Kellan's eye.

"I'm not going to bring that kind of cash to a place where I can't bring some people. For insurance. You know."

Arroyo gave him a long look. "Is it that you do not trust me...or Mr. O'Reilly?"

"Oh, I've built up plenty of trust with Rick. That's

not a problem. But we've never done a deal at this level, either. I've never done a deal with you."

"You would not be doing it with me."

Linn shifted. They had to do it with him. So far El Peligroso hadn't been caught because he never got his hands dirty. He supplied his distributors with top-quality Colombian cocaine, but didn't participate in the transactions himself. But if CLEU wanted to take him down, they had to get the product from his own hands, with witnesses.

"Mr. O'Reilly will take care of the transaction," Arroyo said, as though Mr. O'Reilly were going to do nothing more serious than give them a ride back to San Francisco.

"Then the deal's off." Kellan pushed his coffee away.

Linn sucked in a breath.

"What are you talking about?" O'Reilly demanded. "Mr. Arroyo didn't fly all the way up here from South America so you could flake at the last minute."

"He didn't fly up here to hand the deal over to you, either." He turned to Arroyo. "Either you treat me with the same level of respect as you treat Rick, or we don't do business."

Silence lengthened in the bright dining room while Arroyo weighed two and a half million dollars against the risks.

"Very well," he said at last. "I will conduct this business myself. Here."

Kellan shook his head. "No can do. We'll do it in

San Francisco. Someplace neutral, like a hotel. For all I know, the cops could be onto this place already, and there'll be a nice posse waiting for me when I show up with the money."

"This location is secure." Arroyo's lips had thinned and his voice had become tight. But his fingers on the china handle of his coffee cup were still loose, his movements controlled. Linn wondered just how far they could push him before his patience and caution snapped and they lost everything they'd worked for.

"You can't know that," Kellan replied. "I didn't see any signs of the usual security."

"I have people watching instead of equipment. Everyone on this estate is handpicked by me personally. They have been very effective in keeping it secure."

So the employees were in on it. Some of them were talented at wine making, Linn was sure, but for all she knew, they were processing cocaine in the cellars instead of grapes.

Arroyo went on, "I have a talented vintner, and he has won many legitimate awards. But his talents are not restricted merely to grapes."

Bingo.

Which made it all the more urgent that they set up the deal on neutral ground. They were badly outnumbered here, and had no hope of setting up a team to protect them or to gather evidence.

"I don't like it," Kellan said. "I prefer a hotel. That way we're not likely to attract attention, everyone is on neutral ground, and most important, we don't draw police attention to your operation here."

Arroyo's spoon clinked sharply against the side of his cup as he stirred sugar into it. "What makes you think we will not attract attention in the city?"

"I'll book a room at one of the conference centers. There are so many suits in briefcases walking around that one or two more won't be noticed."

"They will notice five hundred kilos of cocaine, my friend."

"Ah, but that's where your experience comes in. Wine is delivered to hotels all the time. You can plan a delivery, and no one will remark on a winery truck at the loading dock. Only, the cases will be filled with the product. Once you have the cash in hand, and the shipment has been inspected, one of my people can simply direct your driver to my warehouse, unload, and send the truck on its legitimate way."

Arroyo gazed at Kellan thoughtfully.

"It worked for Hidalgo Martinez," Linn put in, sipping her mimosa as if she didn't care much either way. "Only in his case it was carved figurines, of course."

Arroyo turned his impenetrable gaze from her to O'Reilly, and she held her breath while he spoke to his lieutenant. "Do you have someone on the dock at one of the hotels?"

O'Reilly nodded. "The Santo Domingo. And it so happens it's attached to the conference center."

The black eyes flicked back to Kellan. "I will give this some thought. I will let you know."

"I propose a toast, then." Linn smiled and picked up the pitcher of mimosa. "To a successful business relationship."

## 13

THE TAXI DROPPED Linn and Kellan in the center of town, and within five minutes the surveillance van cruised up beside them and the side door slid open.

Kellan handed in their bags, waited for Linn to buckle in, and then swung onto the seat beside her.

"How's the jet-setters, then?" Danny navigated out of town and accelerated onto the freeway.

Linn leaned back on the headrest. "Darling, you'll never get into Eton with an accent like that. It's positively East End."

"Yeah, well, the closest I ever got to Britain was watching *Monty Python*."

"Will the real Linn Nichols please stand up?" Kellan put in. "You can ditch the accent. You're among friendlies."

"The friendlies could use a plan about now, after frying our brains in the heat for two days," Cooper said from the back of the van.

"Be glad it wasn't the whole weekend." Linn's eyes were still closed.

"Yeah, what was up with that?" Danny glanced over his shoulder and back at the highway. "I thought the house party lasted until Sunday. I'm glad it didn't, mind you. We didn't see a thing except the limo coming in and you guys coming out."

"We had what we needed, so I didn't see much point in sticking around waiting for something to go wrong."

"And nobody questioned you?"

Kellan shook his head. "Once we pinned them down to an agreement, they expected I'd have to take off and start making arrangements."

That was part of it. And part of it was that Arroyo had started to get way too interested in Linn over breakfast. Asking her to dazzle Rick O'Reilly was one thing. He was nothing she couldn't handle. But asking her to set herself up with El Peligroso would take her to a whole different level of danger, one to which he couldn't in good conscience send anyone on his team, even someone as resourceful and creative as Linn had proven herself to be.

No, the real reason he'd wanted out of there right after breakfast was the thought of spending any more time together without this thing between them being resolved.

The lady was seriously talented. Seriously smart.

And he was seriously in trouble.

Right from the beginning of this operation, when he'd seen her working O'Reilly on the hot number, he'd been intrigued. But being with her was like trying to focus a camera—like bringing two disparate halves together to make a whole. And last night had been his first glimpse of that whole.

He'd known she was capable, and she'd worked beside him seamlessly. But the times they'd been together were always in the context of work. At the State's temporary apartment. At the winery. Never on their terms or their turf.

It was no wonder she had backed away. He should have thought it through himself and realized that, in essence, they'd begun under false pretenses. What he needed to do now was find some one-on-one time, because the fact was he wanted to be alone with Linn Nichols, away from drugs and the law enforcement world. Just the two of them, all alone, with some serious exploration of each other on the menu.

Linn straightened and swiveled a little on the van's bench seat. As she did so, her knee nudged his thigh and a jolt of sensation raced up his leg, the way a cat's-paw of wind might riffle the calm surface of a lake.

Definitely some serious exploration, he promised himself.

THEY'D LEFT THE WINERY at eleven in the morning, but between the drive from Napa to the city, the endless debriefing with Lieutenant Bryan, her report, and kicking off the machinery of a major joint-forces operation, it was close to seven by the time Linn got back to her condo.

She stood on the front porch and drank in the dreamy peace of the lawns and trees. The creek rustled in the background, and a pair of ruby-throated hummingbirds duked it out over the purple fronds of her Mexican sage.

Salvia, she reminded herself.

This couldn't be the real world, and yet people spent their entire lives in it completely unaware that there were people like Enrique Arroyo out there.

He had taken her aside just before they'd left Napa, when Kellan had been distracted by someone else. It was nothing personal, he'd said, the words coming out of his well-shaped mouth and bearing no relation whatsoever to his grandfatherly mien. If he found out that she had spoken of him to anyone, or capitalized on her knowledge of the winery in any way except for the upcoming buy, he would start with her parents and continue to eliminate the people she loved until he was convinced of her discretion.

The fact that her imaginary parents lived somewhere in England did not have the effect of lessening her very real fear. The only person who might conceivably understand was Kellan. He'd lived in the underworld and had probably had his family threatened more than once.

For the first time, she was thankful that her parents were rootless nomads who sent her postcards from Tibet and Tallahassee, from Paris and Penetanguishene. Gathering material for his novel, her father always said, with a sidewise grin at her mother. Finding inspiration to paint, her mother would counter, and Linn had to admit that at least that one was valid. Gaia Tillman's paintings had been shown in galleries as geographically scattered as her temporary addresses.

With a sigh that was part relief and part resignation, Linn unlocked the door and set her rolling suit-case upright in the hallway. In the kitchen the message light on the answering machine blinked. She punched the button and, as if she'd conjured her up, she heard her mother.

"Hi, sweetie, hope you're well. Dad and I will be swinging through the old stomping grounds next week. It's Dirk and Michelle's twenty-fifth anniversary party and your birthday, too, so we're cutting things short here in Santa Fe. The show was great, even if I'm not sure about the culture. Too many movie stars. Talk to you later." She signed off with her traditional double kiss.

Great. Maybe Arroyo would get a chance to cap her parents after all, if anything went wrong. And naturally Mom had left no callback number. More often than not she forgot to charge the cell phone, but it would be worth trying to stall them for a week or so. They could detour to Sedona or something just until she wrapped the case and Arroyo was, if not incarcerated, then severely restricted in his movements. As in permanently extradited to Colombia.

The last message was from Kellan, obviously calling from his cell phone after she'd left the office.

"Hey, it's me. I know we talked everything into the ground with Bryan, but if you want to get together and go over anything else, or if you just need to talk about nonwork stuff, I'm available." He dictated his number and hung up while she stared at the machine as if it would spontaneously translate man-speak.

Nonwork stuff? Once they started on that, it could be days—and nights—before they finished.

She poured two fingers of Baileys into one of the small crystal glasses she kept for just that purpose, and folded herself into a corner of the couch, resting her head on an embroidered velvet cushion her mom had brought back from Nepal.

Any other woman would be calling Kellan and taking him up on his offer, not sitting here alone and thinking it to death. But that's what she did, Linn mused. She got a sense of distance by sizing things up mentally, by strategizing and preparing herself.

But did that work with relationships? She was no longer so sure. A Caroline-like character might fling herself into sex with abandon and not a lot of thought for the consequences, yet Linn knew she couldn't do that. Could she take a page from Caroline's book and, well, maybe not fling herself but just walk toward it? That would be a change from always backing away. What she needed to do was commit herself. What she'd been doing was trying Caroline on and then when she got in too deep, changing her mind. She couldn't keep doing this without confusing herself, and it was not fair to Kellan.

He'd called her *fearless*. In some things, she was. But could she take a risk with her heart? That was the reason she was waffling. Because it could very well be that they didn't have much time. In law enforcement, you had no guarantee that the person you cared about would walk out the front door in the morning and come back in at night. Sometimes they didn't.

She hadn't quite realized how brave Natalie Wong was, taking on that kind of relationship. And she'd told her the risks were worth it.

But those were big, long-term risks. What about the little, day-to-day ones? If she and Kellan got involved, they would have to deal with a lot of flak at the office. Maybe one of them would have to give up a job they loved and take a transfer into a different organization. Maybe Kellan himself would decide he'd rather have a dial-a-girl after all, and she'd have invested herself in him for nothing.

She could sit here all night and think about the downside. Or she could do something about it. Talk to him. Be fearless.

Linn got up and put the empty glass in the sink.

Maybe she needed to be a little bit like Caroline here, too, and act before she thought.

KELLAN PARKED THE TRUCK in its assigned slot outside his two-story apartment building and hefted his duffel out of the back. When he let himself in, the apartment struck him the way it always did—as a barracks for a man who was hardly ever there. He'd spent more time at the temporary apartment in the past six months than he had at home. It didn't smell or anything, since he had someone clean it twice a month whether it needed it or not, but given the choice, there were a lot of places he'd rather be.

Someday he'd have a place like Linn's, where

you walked in and actually smelled things like plants and furniture polish and cooking. A place with a bit of land to it and a lawn.

But Kellan hardly ever wasted time thinking about someday when there was so much to think about in the now. He could go and do something productive, like work out, or call Coop and meet him for a beer, or call somebody in his black book for some fast and furious sex.

He didn't want exercise or beer or sex.

Correction. He didn't want exercise or beer. Or sex with just anyone. He wanted it with Linn. Badly. And soon.

More than that, he wanted to know she was all right. Undercover ops burned out an investigator faster than any other tour of duty. She was experienced, he knew that, but not at this level. Who better to talk to than he—the guy she'd been with twenty-four/seven. The guy she'd made love with. The guy who, let's face it, cared about his team members and wanted them well adjusted and alert when they went back on duty.

*Yeah, right.*

The guy who was so hungry for the sight of her after a mere two hours that he was tempted to get back in the truck and drive down the peninsula to her condo. He could see himself, hanging around behind a row of rosebushes hoping she'd come out, like some sick high school crush.

He wanted Linn Nichols and there was no getting around it. Yeah, there were one or two minor regulations about fraternizing on duty. They were about to embark on the final phase of the most important investigation of his career, and he needed to keep a clear head. But those sensible thoughts had no effect on this craving in his blood whenever he thought about her, this need for closeness that he only seemed to experience in those few, hard-won moments with her. And he wanted more of those moments. Many more.

He let the bag fall on the floor in the bedroom and peeled out of the jeans he'd been wearing for what seemed like days, though they'd only left Napa this morning, and tossed them in the corner to start a laundry pile. Then he flopped on the bed and hooked up the phone with two fingers.

After four rings, he realized he was holding his breath, and when her answering machine clicked on and he heard the same canned message he'd heard when he called earlier, he let out a long sigh.

Maybe she'd gone to get groceries. Or maybe she was out with someone. A woman couldn't look like she did and not be beating men off the doorstep with a stick.

He dropped the receiver back into its cradle without leaving a message. He'd already left one. Two would make him look lame.

He lay there for a couple of minutes.

The truth was, he didn't want any more phone conversations. They were starting to remind him of Rick O'Reilly, and he didn't want to be thinking about that when he was talking to Linn.

As if his thoughts had activated it, the phone rang. Maybe she'd picked up his message and was calling back.

"Yeah."

"It's me," Cooper Maxwell said. "Want to come over for a beer? I don't know about you, but I could sure use one."

Kellan hesitated. "Maybe not."

"Got something going? We have a couple of days of downtime until the brass get all the agencies and equipment into place."

"I don't know yet."

"Oh, I get it. The word has gone out, right? Black's Babes are homing in on you?" Coop whistled. "I was telling Danny you must have some kind of phone tree arrangement. One call does it all."

"No." Kellan hoped he didn't sound as annoyed as he felt. "I haven't called anyone. Yet."

"What's the matter? Did they all get old or something? I hear there's a new hire in L.A. Word is that she's hot. Redhead. Legs to die for."

"You have my blessing."

Coop was silent for a moment. "Something's happened to you. Are you sick?"

"Do I have to be sick to want to be alone for a while?"

"If it were anybody else, I'd say no. But not the guy who's been collecting girlfriends since the day he signed on."

"Maybe I want a change of pace."

Another silence. "Okay, I get it now. Something

did happen to you. Just what exactly went on while you and The Girl were overnighting in Napa?"

"What makes you think anything went on?"

"My God. Wait till I tell Danny this. Oh, how the mighty are fallen."

"What are you talking about?"

"You and Nichols. Danny and I had a bet you'd have her in the sack by the end of the operation, but I never thought it would go this far."

"You had a bet I'd sleep with her?" Kellan's stomach hollowed with uneasiness. Linn had been afraid of this. He hadn't thought it was a problem, so he hadn't taken her seriously.

That had obviously been a mistake.

"Odds were pretty long," Coop admitted. "But maybe not, if you've got a thing for her. Do you?"

The fact that he even had to debate whether to tell his best friend was a pretty good clue to the strength of his feelings. He and Coop had never held back when it came to talking about women. There just hadn't been anything to conceal. But now it seemed that everything had to be concealed, especially if Coop and Danny were talking about Linn already. If they actually had something to work with, who knew how far the gossip would go?

Far enough to damage her career? Far enough to hurt her?

"I have a lot of respect for her," Kellan said at last. "Call her The Girl if you want, but she's damn good at what she does. If it hadn't been for her, Arroyo probably wouldn't be talking to me."

"Well, they don't get into CLEU because of their looks," Coop reminded him. "It's nice you respect her and all, but it still doesn't explain why you're not rounding up the usual romantic suspects."

"Maybe I'm just out of gas." Kellan pulled his keys out of the pocket of the jeans on the floor. "Maybe I just want some space."

"And maybe I don't believe you. I better call Danny and tell him the odds on that bet just shortened up."

"I wouldn't do that."

"Is that financial advice, or a threat?"

"Coop, give me a break. You never hassled me like this before."

"You never got serious before. The *R* word never came into the conversation before."

"Romantic?"

"Respect. That's a sure danger sign. You told her in the beginning she had to earn it, just like everybody else."

"And she has. With me, anyway. But if you guys go shooting your mouths off, she may lose it."

"Are you saying we'd sabotage her deliberately?" The note of banter and "let's not take life seriously—ever" that habitually lived in Coop's tone was gone. "What kind of friends do you think we are?"

"The kind I can trust. But like you say, it's never been this way before. Look, I've got to go." Kellan jingled the truck keys in his palm. "There's something I have to do."

LINN HAD JUST DRIED OFF after showering the last of Napa down the drain when she heard the knock on the front door. She grabbed her green bathrobe off its hook and tightened the belt at her waist as she padded across the living room to answer it.

The view through the peephole rocked her back on her heels. Well. Great minds were obviously thinking alike.

And what did that mean?

When she pulled the door open, Kellan took her in from head to foot and then grinned as if he'd been given a gift. "Hey." His smile was dazzling. Lamplight struck his cheekbones and gilded the ends of his eyelashes like something from an old painting. "Mind if I come in?"

"Oh. Right. Sure."

Trust her to stare like a teenager as her crush passed by her locker instead of setting the mood for a seduction. Where was Caroline when she needed her?

"Am I interrupting anything?" He looked around as though he expected to see a party, and people standing around with drinks in their hands.

"No. I just got out of the shower."

"I'm always catching you when you're soaking wet."

"Give me a second and I'll put something on." The leather skirt had worked once before, true to Tessa's prediction. If there really were some cosmic thing going on between that skirt and the universe, it would be a shame to waste it.

She turned, but he stopped her with a hand on her arm. "I like you this way. Complete with bathrobe."

And here she'd always thought men responded to lingerie and garter belts. Well, a good operator improvised and worked with what she had on hand. She settled onto the couch, and he sat beside her, the cushions sinking under his weight.

"Did you really drive down here to give me compliments on my bathrobe? I was going to call you back, you know."

Not quite true. She was going to drive up to his place and give him a night he wouldn't forget. It was sheer luck she'd decided to shower first. If he hadn't been home when she got there, she'd have lost her courage and her opportunity.

But opportunity had knocked right on her own front door.

"I like it." The smile flashed and was gone. "But I didn't come just for that. I talked to Coop."

She eyed him. "Is that good or bad?"

"He wanted to know if something was going on between you and me."

*Did he, now.* "What did you tell him?"

"I told you I wouldn't say anything, so I didn't. I just said I respected you, and left it at that."

Between friends as close as he and Cooper seemed to be, Linn was sure there was more to it. But it was just as likely he wouldn't tell her. She had other things on her mind, anyway—and one of them wasn't talking about Cooper Maxwell.

"Thank you," she said absently. How long would

it take to undo the buttons on his shirt? There was one way to find out. With a subtle movement of her shoulder, the robe fell open a little.

Kellan's gaze followed it, then away. "He…he wanted to know if I was going to call anyone while I had a couple of days of downtime."

Another movement, and the robe slipped off her shoulder altogether. "And are you?"

She played with the top button on his shirt. He seemed to focus on her bare shoulder, as if he were wondering what the robe would do now. The button popped out of its hole and she went to work on the next one.

"I said I wouldn't. Call anyone, I mean."

Two buttons.

"You called me," she said helpfully.

"You're why I'm not calling anyone else."

Something behind her ribs bubbled over, the way champagne does when it's shaken. For the first time, Linn wondered if Natalie was right. Had both of them met their match in the other, and it had just taken them this long to see it? And worse, had they found each other just in time to realize it and then walk into an operation where a simple mistake could be the end of everything?

Three buttons.

"Linn, what are you doing?" A strong hand on her wrist stopped her from managing the fourth button.

"Undoing your shirt."

She'd made up her mind that tonight was going to be stolen out of time, one of those little oases of cold sanity and hot pleasure that they seemed to be able to create out of circumstances that shouldn't allow either one.

But now it seemed much more than that. She'd deliberately chosen him. And he, it appeared, had deliberately chosen her.

"Talk is starting to get around the office. You were right. We can't do this."

His grip loosened, and she worked the fourth button free. The collar of her robe drooped even further, and she felt cool air on her chest from the open sliding glass door. If she looked down to see what she'd revealed, it would spoil the effect. But the expression on his face was as good as a mirror.

Better. She didn't want to see herself as she was, anyway. She wanted to see herself the way he saw her.

The last button gave in to her fingers, and she spread the two halves of his shirt apart, flattening her hand on his chest. "That's more like it."

She no longer cared what everyone in the office thought. Once the talk got started, the truth didn't matter anyway. There was nothing either of them could do about it now, so she wasn't going to let it bother her. There were many more important things to think about.

And do.

"Are you listening?"

"Oh, yes." His skin felt so hot, so solid. She could just run a hand over his pectorals, like this…

"I am trying to do the right thing, here." His

belly was hard, and the muscles flinched under her explorations.

"I appreciate that," she murmured. "But whether you take your shirt off now or not, it isn't going to stop the talk, is it?"

"Well, no, not right now, but it's the principle—"

"I do admire your…principles. Come here."

She leaned over and brushed his hair away from his ear, then touched his earlobe with the tip of her tongue, dampening it. When she nibbled it just the slightest bit, his breathing changed.

She loved being able to do that.

Her leisurely exploration continued down the side of his neck. His mouth had traveled all over her body, but in one of life's great inequities, hers had not had the same pleasure. She planned to balance that right now.

With his buttons undone, it didn't take long for her to pull the shirt out of his waistband and strip it down his arms. She tossed it on the coffee table.

"Just what do you have in mind?" he inquired softly as she tasted the skin over his perfect pecs. But she didn't reply. She'd moved on to the flat cinnamon nipple and bitten it gently.

Oops, there went the breathing again. And it never quite returned to its previous regularity, either, especially when she ran her tongue over his abs and explored the depression of his belly button.

"Linn—"

South of his waistband, she could see the bulge of his erection confined by the fabric of his clean khaki trousers.

And while she was busy looking, he found the opportune moment to act. His fingers tugged at her waist, a draft of cool air traveled the length of her body and her bathrobe landed in a heap on top of his shirt on the coffee table.

"If we were playing strip poker, you'd lose." His cocky grin didn't stay in place for long. She scrambled on top of him, and he landed on his back, stretched out the length of the couch, his head pillowed on a batiked cushion from Bali.

"It's a lucky thing we're not playing, then, isn't it?"

No more playing anything—whether it was parts or games. Dean and Caroline were far away, and in this room there were only the two of them as they really were.

At last.

Linn slipped her arms around his neck and looked down into his eyes. His hands slid upward over her bare skin and he circled her waist, moving slowly, each caress a discovery.

"I'm not playing," he told her, his gaze serious. "But I couldn't tell Coop."

"Do you normally tell him everything?" she whispered against his lips.

"Usually there's nothing to tell. But now when there is, I couldn't say anything."

"Tell me." She tasted his lower lip, running her tongue along its fullness. When he opened his mouth to her, she deepened the kiss and explored the warmth inside.

"After," he managed, then pulled her head down. Now it was her turn to kiss him with all the passion fizzing in her blood, the kind of kiss that made arrows of desire shoot from mouth to breast to clitoris. The kind of kiss that made him lift his hips in suggestion, grinding his erection against her pelvic bones in a way that made her breathless with anticipation for more.

He broke the kiss and nuzzled her throat, possessing each inch with his mouth before moving on to the next, as if creating a necklace of moisture on her skin. When he arrived at the first swell of her breast, he grasped her around the waist and scooted her up a little. She braced her elbows on the pillow and let her nipple brush his lips.

Now it was her turn for a hitch in the breathing. Her breasts were aching for him, her nipples distended and so sensitive that each brush of his tongue was exquisite torture. His lips traveled the landscape of each breast with equal care, his tongue swirling where it would make her gasp, and he bared his teeth to nibble where it would make her moan.

How well he knew her now. Or maybe it was how well she'd allowed him to know her. He'd been able to make her focus on him and think about sex from the very beginning, to the exclusion of everything else and practically jeopardizing her ability to do her job. Now it seemed as though that focus had grown to the point that her whole world had narrowed down to this one moment, this one man.

He scooted her up his body again, and suddenly she saw where he was going. He smiled up at her, a challenging, dangerous look, and before she could pull away or rethink the situation or even react, he'd grasped her waist with both hands and positioned her above him.

With her knees sinking into the couch cushions on either side of his shoulders, she looked down into his face. The desire humming through her blood seemed to pool between her legs, producing a creamy trickle of arousal.

She wanted this. Oh, yes. Any lingering thought of pulling away vanished like a puff of steam.

He pulled her toward him and her back arched in anticipation as he parted her folds with sure fingers. His tongue found the moisture between her legs and licked it up, and he grasped her buttocks to pull her closer. Every sense she possessed zeroed in on his tongue and what it could do to her. She was hardly aware of bracing both hands on the arm of the couch, because her body was a wave of pleasure, ebbing and flowing as his skillful tongue intensified the pressure and backed it away.

"Kellan, I need—"

"I know what you need."

Then he had mercy on her, his strokes centering on her clit, licking and savoring every molecule of her pleasure. In an explosion of sensation, her orgasm blossomed, and she bucked against his mouth, hardly aware that his hands still held her in place, trapping her where she most wanted to be.

Gasping, she fell to one side, and he was there to catch her, to roll her under him. Impatiently she undid his belt and pulled at his trousers so that he was as naked as she was. Her mouth was hungry for whatever part of him she could reach, her very skin craving his warmth and weight.

"One second—" He grabbed his pants and, with his arms around her as he scrabbled through the pockets, found a condom.

She helped him on with it and, at last, time seemed to slow as her legs parted around his thighs and she raised her hips to meet him in welcome. He slid into her body with exquisite slowness.

There was no question of backing away or of trying to do the right thing. The right thing was here and now. As Kellan moved, slowly at first and then with increasing urgency, she felt the pleasure build inside again. His breathing changed and she knew he was as close as she, and then she could no longer sense the outside world. All her awareness centered on him as he buried his face in her breasts and muffled his cry against her skin.

And knowing she had brought him such pleasure tilted her over the edge a second time. She gripped his shoulders, shuddering with the force of it. When the waves had subsided and she could breathe, she found that they were tightly wrapped around each other in the deep cushions of the couch.

SHE MUST HAVE FALLEN ASLEEP, because somewhere in the dark and the silence of the early hours of the morning, she heard a whisper above her that said, "I'll talk to you later today."

When she woke, the sunlight was pouring in through the still-open sliding glass door, and she was stretched out on the couch.

Alone.

"Kellan?" A quick search of the condo confirmed it. He hadn't stayed. This was a switch. He'd done the backing away, even though it was no longer what she wanted.

Linn walked slowly into the bathroom, the tiles cold under her bare feet, and turned on the shower, half hoping it would be like a magic signal that would bring him back. She opened the cabinet where she kept her soap and stepped back, startled, as a silver rain of little foil packets fell out of it.

Two or three landed in her hand, and her fingers closed around them.

Okay, so he was gone. But only temporarily.

When she climbed into the shower, she was smiling.

# *14*

THE CALL CAME IN late Thursday afternoon to the "hot number," and Kellan took it in his role as Dean. When it was over and the technician indicated it had come from one of O'Reilly's new cell phones in the vicinity of the Transamerica Building, Kellan waved the team into one of the interview rooms.

"He was probably visiting his broker," Coop said wryly. "Or setting up a fake corporation or something."

"Or he had a meeting with that guy who used to do the financials for that computer company," Linn said. "Farley. Arroyo's money guy."

"Which would make sense, given that they're expecting two and a half mil tomorrow night." Kellan gave her an approving glance, and Linn resisted the urge to reach out and run her palm up his bare arm. Instead she put her hands in her lap, one imprisoned inside the other.

This was awful. This was why she'd stuck to the "no hands" policy in her work relationships for the past several years. Keeping her hands to herself wasn't the problem—she had pretty healthy survival instincts. But her whole body, her skin, her muscles—probably even her hair—right now they all wanted to be close to Kellan.

Whole-body yearning.

This was exactly how addicts felt, from all accounts, and if she indulged the urge, the mortality rate might be just as high. Once they were out there on the mean streets, one hesitation, one moment of fear on behalf of the other, could mean sudden death for both Kellan and her. Gritting her teeth, Linn shook the grim thoughts away, took courage from Natalie's advice and the thought of what Kellan had left behind in her bathroom cabinet, and laced her fingers together more tightly.

In the chair beside her at the conference table, Kellan resumed the briefing. "Okay, so the Santo Domingo is a go. Eleven o'clock tomorrow night. We've got two suites reserved, one where we'll do the deal, and the one adjoining it where the team will be stationed."

"What's the layout?" Danny wanted to know.

"The ventilation system runs right above the two rooms. There's a vent on one side that's the twin of a vent on the team's side. It'll do for the audio. Just keep in mind they'll probably do a sweep themselves."

"Are you wearing a wire?"

"Definitely. I think I've established enough of a rep with Arroyo that he won't pat me down. I'll be on one channel, and Linn will be on the other. Control will relay information between us."

"What do you mean, between you?" Danny asked.

"She's not going in with me."

Heads swiveled to look at her as she straightened in the chair. "What?" She couldn't have heard correctly.

"What I said. You know as well as I do that Arroyo isn't going to do this with a woman around."

Adrenaline hit Linn's bloodstream like a splash of scalding ice water. After all the work they'd done together, after all the crap she'd had to endure from O'Reilly, he wasn't going to let her in on the final scene?

"Who's going to back you up, then?" she demanded.

"Coop is."

Cooper looked from her to Kellan as if he didn't know whether to be happy about this or not.

"He'll play the money guy," Kellan continued. "He'll flash the cash at them but never actually take it out of the briefcase. The taxpayers' money has to go back into the Treasury once we're done."

"So what do you expect me to do?" Linn wasn't finished with him yet. There was nothing more aggravating than a man with a logical, reasonable plan. Especially one in which she'd had no input. He was doing it again. Taking away her choices when he knew how much this meeting—not to mention his safety—meant to her. She could give in when it meant Chinese food, but not when so much was riding on their partnership.

"Your job will be to make sure they get to the dock

with the kilos," Kellan told her. "Once I have the okay from you via cell phone that the shipment's there, we'll break the news to Arroyo and O'Reilly that they're invited to a long vacation in the federal pen." He grinned, as if he'd just handed her a present and couldn't wait to see if she liked it.

It was perfect. Reasonable. Necessary.

It stank.

She'd be half a dozen floors or more away from him when the deal went down. If something went wrong, he could die of a bullet wound long before she would even know about it, much less get there in time to do something.

*Wait a minute.* She forced herself to sit back in the chair.

This wasn't the concern of one team member for another. This wasn't even the usual pregame jitters. This was the panic of a woman for the safety of her man.

Linn sat motionless while the knowledge seeped into her bones and the team argued all around her about firepower and logistics and surveillance equipment.

There was no more backing away now. She'd fallen well and truly in love with him.

With a big, devastating, annoyingly logical man who could melt her with a smile or even a word, and who'd proven it oh so many times over in the last few days.

Now what was she going to do?

"SO, HOW DO I LOOK?"

In the spare room of the temporary house, Cooper

stood in front of the mirror and tugged on the hem of his jacket. He turned, looked behind him and shrugged his shoulders to make it drape properly.

"Like a wiseguy." Kellan fastened a heavy gold chain around his neck. It had been rented for his final appearance as Dean, with a hefty insurance rider. "I like these collarless shirts. No tie."

"I have a personal rule. No ties except at last rites and in court. No exceptions."

"Last rites?"

"Yeah. Weddings." Coop grinned, a grin that meant he was about to lean on the ropes of their friendship and test them. "Speaking of which, what's new with you and Linn?"

"Nothing."

Coop snorted and tucked his service weapon into a shoulder holster under his suit jacket. "Yeah, right. You look at each other and the oxygen practically combusts in the air. You tell her she's not in the deal and she looks like she's going to blow a gasket. Sure signs of nothing, in my book."

Carefully not looking at his buddy, Kellan pulled his shirt out a little so it would hide any evidence of the transmitter taped to his ribs. "She wants to be involved, that's all."

"Yeah. Involved with you."

"What's so bad about that?"

Cooper gave him a sideways look. "You shouldn't shit in your own backyard, man."

Kellan wondered if anyone had ever written up Cooper Maxwell for the language he used on duty.

"You're her team lead," Coop went on. "Where do you think you're going to go with this? And don't give me that look. Danny and I haven't been talking. The whole team knows."

They did? "Yeah, well, if the team knows, they can just stay away from her."

Coop snorted again. "Most of us don't like to make love with a whip in one hand and a chair in the other. You've got no competition from me."

"She's not like that once you get to know her. She's smart and creative, and damn good at her job."

"So you said. And I know it, too," Coop allowed. "But she's one of ours. Not the usual out-of-towner."

Kellan thought briefly about telling him to mind his own business, but that was like telling his sisters to keep a secret. It would only escalate to teasing and pranks and succeed in making Linn's life miserable.

"If you're done reviewing the policy manual, it's time to go buy some cocaine."

Two local DEA agents and a couple of the plainclothes guys from San Francisco PD sat in the living room, but they weren't reviewing the files Kellan had left on the table. They were flirting uproariously with Linn, who was dressed in an eye-popping pair of black suede jeans, a red tank top and a black leather bomber jacket. She was holding court with as much aplomb as Caroline, and the men were eating it up.

"Everybody ready to go?" he asked loudly.

One of the agents grinned at him. "Whenever you are. Investigator Nichols has just been briefing us."

Any of these yo-yos were entitled to ask her out, he thought sourly, once the operation was over. She could have her choice of any single man in the room, but he planned to be the one she chose. As soon as tonight was finished, he'd find a way to stop her from running.

But he had to put thoughts like that out of his mind and focus on the job at hand. Once they had Arroyo and O'Reilly in the bag, he could think about how he was going to show Linn he was the man for her.

They departed the temporary house in small teams, five minutes apart. Linn and Danny went in one car, shadowed by a backup vehicle, to take up positions at the hotel's loading dock and wait for the winery truck. At this time of night there would be few deliveries, and the chances of someone innocently dropping off a load of bagels and getting caught in the crossfire would be low. The DEA guys were headed to the surveillance room at the hotel. It was a carefully choreographed dance, played out in one form or another by narcotics teams all across the country.

Which didn't make it any less personal.

A CLEU member dropped them under the portico at the hotel before parking down the street to give them the heads-up when Arroyo arrived. Kellan and Cooper, who was carrying the briefcase containing the State's hundred-thousand-dollar flash roll, strolled through the lobby and rode the elevator up to the eighth floor.

Cooper slid the briefcase into a drawer in the suite's entertainment center and closed it. Certain his heart was pumping sixty percent adrenaline, forty percent blood, Kellan paced through the suite's sitting room from the windows to the door and back, while Coop did the same in the bedroom, circling the computer desk again and again.

The wireless transmitter in his ear clicked. "Control to Team One," said the calm voice of the radio operator. "The perimeter team advises your target has arrived. Front portico, late-model luxury sedan. ETA three minutes."

"What about Team Two, Control?" he asked.

"No sign of the delivery van as yet."

The racing adrenaline settled into cool, focused control. By the time the soft knock came at the door, Kellan's jitters had stopped.

He opened it to see a small crowd composed of Arroyo and his four bodyguards. Arroyo nodded as he passed him in the narrow hallway.

"I hope you are well?"

"Never better."

Two of the bodyguards stayed outside, one standing next to the door and one opposite the elevator. And Kellan had no doubt whatsoever that everyone was armed to the teeth.

El Peligroso wanted to make sure he was in control of the deal.

The U.S. of A. was a free country. He could think that if he wanted to.

"Gentlemen," he said with a killer smile as he walked into the sitting room. "Let's do a little business, shall we?"

DANNY'S ESPRESSO smelled more and more tempting the longer they sat in the dark. Linn wished she'd let him get one for her, too, when they'd stopped at the coffee bar, but the problem with drinking coffee on stakeouts with guys was that they got to relieve themselves practically wherever they wanted, and she had to go find a gas station or convenience store, sometimes blocks away.

And there was no way she was going to be caught in the ladies' room when five hundred kilos of cocaine rolled into the shipping dock.

So she sat in the passenger seat while the scent of coffee and the itch of the transmitter taped to her ribs drove her slowly crazy, and endured the mixture of worry, frustration and adrenaline zooming around in her stomach. It spiked when a delivery truck turned the corner and rumbled up to the dock, but the sign on the side was for the local newspaper. Both Linn and Danny subsided into their seats, watching as the dock attendant received the bundles of the early-morning edition, tossing them onto the concrete as if they weighed nothing.

"Think that's our guy?" Danny said.

Linn checked the photograph. "Looks like it. Control," she said, "I'm confirming O'Reilly's man is on the dock."

"Roger that," the operator replied in the tiny transmitter in her left ear.

Danny drained the last of the coffee, for which she was grateful. Now she wouldn't ask him for a sip, which was friendlier than she wanted to get with a co-worker. Danny was nice enough, but he wasn't Kellan.

"So," Danny said, apropos of nothing. "After this, there's no more Dean and Caroline, eh?"

Danny's gaze drifted idly from the now-deserted dock to the point on the long alley where the winery truck would turn into the loading area, then moved to her waist, where it rested a second longer than necessary.

"No," she said blankly. "They'll die a natural death, I suppose."

"Too bad. Coop had twenty dollars on them together by the time we closed this case."

Linn forced herself not to react. After all, she and Kellan had chosen each other despite the rules against it. She just wished Danny hadn't picked a moment when at least a dozen people were listening in on their channel.

"Tell Coop he'd do better putting his money in a retirement account." Her lips felt tight on the words. Kellan had respected her enough not to talk about their relationship, even to his closest friends. But it was so guylike for his friends to take her on, not in private, but in a very public forum.

A challenge. A dare.

"I did," Danny said, as if it didn't matter very

much. "But you know Cooper. He never listens to me. He figures they're a good match."

"How does he figure that?" She shouldn't encourage him. But how to shut him up?

"Well, she's different, isn't she?"

He was talking about Caroline as if she were real. Was it some kind of code? Or was he just going to make a complete fool of her in the ears of everyone monitoring their conversation?

"Not his usual. Nope, not at all."

Was that a good thing? Did this mean his friends approved? Linn waited for the other shoe to drop.

Instead, Danny went on, "Isn't it weird trying to maintain a character that's so unlike you?"

For a moment Linn had to regroup, realizing he was asking her a direct question. She was tempted to say no. She'd embraced her inner Caroline and was actually starting to enjoy it. Flirting with the feds back in the temporary house had been a hoot. She'd even gone out and bought leather pants, something she would never have dreamed of doing a month ago. Maybe a flavoring of Caroline did a woman's character good. But this wasn't the kind of thing you admitted to a fellow investigator on your very first stakeout together.

"Sometimes," she said at last. It wasn't a very satisfactory answer, but it was better than the truth. Tessa had told her she needed to integrate her sexy side—her inner bad girl—into her personality, and she'd been right. Caroline had a helluva lot more fun than Linn did. Once this was over, it was going to be interesting see where else Caroline planned to take her. She could really get to like it.

"Heads up," Danny said quietly. "Team Two to Control. The van's here."

"Ten-four. Will advise Team One."

The delivery van from the winery cruised slowly up the street with only its parking lights on. It reversed into the loading dock and came to a stop at the bottom of the ramp.

"Let's do this," Linn said, and reached for the door handle.

Danny grabbed her arm. "Wait a minute. What's he doing here?"

Linn searched the stark light and shadow of the dock and watched a big man leap down from the passenger side of the van with unexpected agility.

"Dammit," she said. "Control, Rick O'Reilly is in the van. He's supposed to be in the hotel room doing the deal with Arroyo."

"So what made him change his plans?" Danny asked.

O'Reilly was walking toward their car.

Linn shouldered the door open. "Looks like we're about to find out."

# 15

LINN WAS PREPARED to let O'Reilly take his time kissing her in greeting, but to her surprise the gesture was short and businesslike. She gave him a megawatt smile as she pulled away.

"Darling. I've missed you."

O'Reilly glanced from her to Danny. "Likewise. Who's this?"

*Likewise?* This wasn't the hungry predator of the weekend, taking advantage of the fact that Kellan wasn't around. This was a man who had moved on. But she didn't have time to wonder why. Maybe he got like this when he conducted business.

"A friend of Dean's. Danny, this is Richard O'Reilly, Mr. Arroyo's man." Danny nodded, close-lipped. "Danny's here to do the heavy lifting for me."

"There's plenty to lift." O'Reilly motioned them toward the dock, where the guy they'd seen before was already unloading crates onto a pallet jack. "We are making a legitimate wine delivery. Dean's product is under it."

"Once we've confirmed the shipment is in order, the winery truck will go to the warehouse. We'll ride along." Linn allowed Danny to boost her up onto the concrete dock. "Dean will finalize arrangements with Mr. Arroyo upstairs."

And they would drive the van full of cocaine straight to the impound yard at headquarters and unload the kilos into the exhibit cage, to be held for evidence at Arroyo and O'Reilly's trial.

While Arroyo's man and the van driver unloaded the legitimate cases of wine, she stood idly by, half listening to O'Reilly try to get a conversation out of Danny, and half reading the headlines on the stack of newspapers that still stood, unattended, on the concrete.

Governor's Tax Proposal Passes.

Nasdaq Indicates Computer Market on the Upswing.

Drug Suspect Found Dead in Dade County Home.

Baby Escapes Death in Overheated Car.

What?

The plastic strap holding the bundle of papers in a stack had slipped when it landed, so Linn had no trouble extracting a thick copy from the haphazard pile.

Businessman Hidalgo Martinez, accused of importing more than one hundred pounds of wholesale pure cocaine into Miami Beach on his yacht, was found dead in his Boca Raton home yesterday morning by his housekeeper. Sources say that Martinez had cut a deal with federal prosecutors wherein he would name names in exchange for a reduction in his charges, but a representative of the Department of Justice was not available for comment.

Linn let the paper fall onto the stack with a slap. "Control, new information," she murmured. "Hidalgo Martinez is dead. Tell Team One to watch their backs. We've been made."

"I AM ASSUMING you do not have two and a half million dollars in your possession," El Peligroso said, pinching the legs of his fine wool trousers as he seated himself in the chair with a view of the door.

"You're correct," Kellan said just as smoothly. "I see your financier has brought his laptop. This is merely earnest money, to show our honest intentions. As soon as I have word from my people at the dock that the shipment is in order, I'll have Mr. Cooper initiate the wire transfer into any account you choose to name."

Arroyo nodded. "That will be satisfactory. The days of carrying suitcases of cash in a suspicious manner are, *de gracias a Dios,* gone forever."

"Would you like to see it?" Cooper said. He flipped open the latches and opened the glossy briefcase. Rows of bundled bills lay inside. "Five percent in advance."

Arroyo inclined his head. "I am less interested in your intentions than in your actions," he said. "We will wait for word from downstairs."

The device in Kellan's ear clicked. "Team One,"

said the operator, "problems. Rick O'Reilly is down at the dock. Team Two reports that Hidalgo Martinez is dead. It's possible you've been compromised. Recommend caution."

Their informant was dead? And what was Tricky Ricky doing at the dock? Arroyo wouldn't have sent his first lieutenant to do something as menial as unloading product; he had four goons right here for that. But if Hidalgo had been taken out, that meant somehow Arroyo's organization had learned he'd flipped. It was a given that before he died, he'd have told them everything he could in hopes of saving his skin. The guy who'd ratted out the organization in the first place would rat out the police without a second's hesitation if he thought it would buy him even a few minutes of time.

But for Hidalgo, evidently, time had run out.

If Arroyo had sent Rick O'Reilly along with the shipment, it meant he was there for something serious.

Such as murder.

Kellan pasted on a smile and turned back to Arroyo, hoping his color was normal. He had to wrap this up and get down to the dock. Once O'Reilly knew Linn had no value to either Arroyo or his career, God knew what he'd do to her.

His phone trilled twice and went silent, the agreed-upon signal for the van's arrival, since Arroyo could not know they were communicating electronically.

"The shipment has arrived." He glanced from Arroyo to Farley, the money guy. "We should receive confirmation of its contents shortly."

"Ah." Arroyo sounded happy, as if he'd been told dinner would be served in the lounge. "We can begin the preliminaries for the transaction, at least. Mr. Farley, your computer?"

Farley flipped open the laptop, plugged the modem jack into the phone on the desk and waited for it to boot up.

Kellan felt the adrenaline in his bloodstream heat up again and begin its tap dance along his veins. Of course there was no money to transfer. The hundred thousand in the flash roll was meant to convince, not to leave his custody. He needed to hear from Linn about the shipment before the guy got the bank interface up, or he was going to have to stall.

If it really was Arroyo's intention to kill him and Coop, it would happen once the wire transfer was underway. Once the Colombian had the money, there was no reason to leave them alive.

Except for the team in the next room. The arrests would be fast, but Kellan doubted the ambulances would get here in time to let him enjoy them.

As soon as he knew the shipment was all there, he was going to have to arrest Arroyo and Farley and render the goons nonop. Two against four—at least until the team kicked the door down.

*Come on, Linn,* he urged her wordlessly. *Get it done and let me know you're safe.*


"THAT'S THE WINE, THEN," the driver told O'Reilly. "What do you want me to do now?"

O'Reilly glanced at Linn, and she smiled Caroline's catlike smile at him. He glanced away. "Nothing. The customer will check the merchandise, and you'll be on your way."

Something was definitely wrong. There was no emotion at all in that glance.

Linn thought fast. How else could he operate? From her observations, he fit the profile of a sociopath. He would have to reduce his victims to objects in order to kill them, then figure out some way of rationalizing it for himself, or it would drive him mad. That soulless glance confirmed her worst fears. If Hidalgo had informed on them before he died, she and Kellan and everyone associated with them tonight were simply to be taken out.

It was a damn good bet O'Reilly hadn't actually bothered to pack the shipment.

"Dan, give me a hand, would you?" she asked. A good look in Danny's eyes told her he'd arrived at the same conclusions as she had. They were going to have to come up with a plan on the fly.

She just wished she knew what it was.

"Start with this one, if you like." O'Reilly indicated the nearest crate with a wave of his hand. The driver handed him a short crowbar and Danny levered off the lid with a screech of nails.

Nestled in hollows in the packing material were neat one-kilo packages wrapped in brown plastic. Over Danny's shoulder she did a swift count.

"Twelve kilos per crate?" she asked O'Reilly.

"Give or take," he replied. "Forty crates."

"Danny, check another one, just to be thorough,

will you?" She strolled over to O'Reilly and slipped her arm through his. "And what are you doing after our business is concluded here?"

Her left breast rubbed his arm. When he looked down at her, the soulless look left his eyes and something else slowly took its place. Something that was ugly and frightening, but at least it was alive.

"What, you're not going to your warehouse?" he asked.

She waved a negligent hand. "Heavens, no. How dull. I can't imagine you'd be interested in this sort of thing, either. Why don't we leave the details to our very capable people here, and go and have a drink? After all, I think we have something to celebrate."

"What's Dean going to think if you do that?"

"Dean," she said tightly, "is so wrapped up in impressing El Peligroso that he'll hardly have time to wonder where I've gone. And you've already earned your stripes, haven't you?" She ran a finger down the open placket of his shirt. "You don't need to waste your time toadying to the boss. You can afford to leave that to the people who are—" she paused, as if searching for the right word, and heard Danny murmur something to the van driver "—less secure than you are. In more ways than one."

"You are so right," he said softly. "I knew you'd come around."

Over his shoulder she glanced at Danny. Even in the shadows of the truck, which was illuminated by a single bulb mounted overhead, she could see his face was stark and white. He moved his head sharply to the right, then back.

The crate was empty.

"Darling," she whispered against O'Reilly's lips, and kneed him hard in the groin.

THE PHONE TRILLED a second time, and Arroyo smiled tightly as Kellan flipped it open.

"The van did not contain the shipment," murmured the operator in his ear. "Except for a decoy crate. Fake the transaction. Get the target to commit himself."

Kellan stiffened with apprehension and a flood of fear for Linn that he couldn't under any circumstances allow his features to show. He couldn't even ask Control if Linn and Danny were safe. If the shipment was a fake and O'Reilly was down there, Kellan had been right. Every second mattered. But he was trapped here as surely as if the doors were locked. Until they secured Arroyo, he couldn't do what his heart demanded he do, which was protect the woman he loved from the immediate threat.

The woman he loved.

Between one second and the next, Kellan realized his life had changed. For the first time, there was someone whose survival was even more important to him than his own.

The problem was, he had no control over what was happening eight floors down. And if there was anything he hated, it was not having control, not being able to plan for any eventuality, not being the point man for what went down.

For the next few minutes, at least, he was going to have to trust Linn's skill at her job. To keep them all alive, he had to behave as if there was nothing wrong and just trust that she and everyone else on his team knew what to do.

For him, nothing was more difficult.

He looked up and met Arroyo's smile with one of his own, wolfishly insincere. "Well, gentlemen, it appears as though the merchandise has arrived safely, and everything's in order."

Arroyo sat back. "I have fulfilled my obligations. Mr. Cooper, initiate your transaction, please."

Farley got up, and Coop glanced at Kellan as he passed him and took his place in front of the laptop. Instead of watching over Coop's shoulder as he brought up his personal credit union's Web site on the screen, Kellan circled around between Arroyo and the nearest goon.

"You don't need me any longer, so I'll say goodbye here, and take the shipment to my warehouse myself."

"Transaction's in progress," Cooper reported, glancing from the screen to Farley, who was looking a little puzzled.

"I'm afraid that won't be possible, Mr. Wilcox," Arroyo said, regret in his voice. "I'm afraid I must tell you some very sad news."

Kellan felt the floor vibrate, as if an earthquake tremor—enough to make the plants shake, say—had rolled through.

"Target at the elevator is nonop," reported Control. "Advancing on the door."

"I am afraid your lovely Caroline will be devastated to hear that she will never be a guest in the home of Hidalgo Martinez again."

Kellan lifted his eyebrows. Here it was. "Why, has he been sentenced already? I thought the hearing wasn't for a year or more."

"He has met with a more efficient judicial system than that of the United States government, Mr. Wilcox. He has met with me. He betrayed me, and now he has been punished."

"Betrayed you? How?" Kellan braced himself for what was about to happen.

"He lied to me. He said that you were a friend, and reliable."

"I'm both."

"I am not a fool, Mr. Wilcox."

"Transaction complete," Coop said helpfully.

"Hey, I don't think—" Farley started to say, leaning toward the laptop, but Arroyo overrode him.

"Or should I refer to you as Investigator Black of the California Law Enforcement Unit?"

The words, chipped out of ice, were no sooner out of his mouth than the door banged inward and half a dozen people belonging to an alphabet soup of state and federal agencies exploded into the room.

THE LAST THING KELLAN HEARD before he was hustled out of the room by his security team was two DEA guys duking it out with the INS over who actually got custody of Arroyo. He'd put his life on hold for six months to roam the streets as Dean Wilcox, whose only goal had been to bring down Rick O'Reilly and, with him, the famous El Peligroso. Funny how he didn't care right now who got the credit and who got to fill out the paperwork.

All he cared about was reaching Linn, and the security team charged with his safety didn't seem to get that. While Control dished out staccato commands in his ear, directing each arm of the operation, he tried to get a word in edgewise. All he needed was ten minutes. Just ten minutes, and then he'd vacate the site like a good investigator.

Finally there was nothing left to do but pull rank. A minute later Kellan ducked through the hotel's massive, stainless-steel kitchen and skidded out onto the loading dock.

"Kell." Danny Kowalski was standing on the hydraulic tailgate of the winery truck. "Over here."

Around him, the team was cleaning up. A guy struggled under a CLEU agent on the far side of the dock, amid toppled bundles of newspapers. Someone else had a guy in a dark jacket up against the door. He leaped into the back of the winery truck.

"Where's Linn?" he demanded.

"Right here."

He heard her, but he couldn't see her. All he saw were a pair of men's boots sticking out from behind a pile of crates.

"Are you okay?" He jumped another crate and landed beside the boots, then gawked down at the floor.

Rick O'Reilly was out cold, facedown on the

wet metal, and Linn sat on his butt. She took his un-resisting arm and snapped the second handcuff around his wrist.

"I'd have to say I've never been better," she said with satisfaction. "There. Control, loading dock secure. We're coming in." She glanced at Danny and Kellan. "Why don't you two see if you can get him into a vehicle?"

She was all right. O'Reilly had obviously tried something on her, but she'd won. "Did you do this?"

Danny picked up O'Reilly's feet and gestured for Kellan to do the same with the guy's shoulders. He must have weighed two hundred pounds—uncon-scious, it seemed like three.

"She kneed him in the balls and coldcocked him with a bottle of wine," Danny grunted. They hefted O'Reilly off the tailgate and into the nearest un-marked vehicle. "Get out the whip and chair. That woman scares me."

Kellan grinned. That was his girl. "No kidding."

"Doesn't she scare you?"

Kellan glanced over his shoulder, where Linn was giving instructions about the disposition of the truck and its cargo, with one finger on the transmitter in her ear as if it were talking at the same time.

"I like a woman who kicks butt and takes names."

Danny rolled his eyes. "Watch yourself. The next name she takes might be yours."

Linn jumped down from the tailgate and walked toward them, her black suede jeans hugging her hips and thighs, her jacket riding easily on her shoulders.

Kellan's heart jerked in his chest when she smiled as though he was the one person on earth she most wanted to see.

"That's the plan, Danny," he said softly. "That is definitely the plan."

# 16

THE DRIVE DOWN Highway 101 to Linn's San Mateo condo took about ten minutes as opposed to the usual twenty or twenty-five. There was no one on the road at this time of night, and Kellan blew the carbon out of Victor-21's high-performance engine like it had never been blown before.

Before he'd signed his equipment back in at the office, he'd learned from Control that Linn hadn't yet done so and she still had preliminary reports to finish.

Reports could wait. As far as he was concerned, he and Linn couldn't.

He was waiting on the front steps of her condo, listening to the birds wake up in the crepe myrtle across the road when the garage door rolled up and her little SUV came around the corner and parked inside.

Instead of going through the house, she came outside and walked up the steps to meet him. Her eyes were somber, with the pinched look of sleep deprivation. Her skin looked fragile, or maybe it was just that its normal color had faded under all the stress and exhaustion of the night.

Without a word he took her in his arms. One hand caressed her shoulder blades, her ribs, slid down to her hip. Taking inventory. Making sure everything was there and she was all right.

"This has been the longest night of my life," he said at last.

In a nearby tree, a bird let loose with a piercing trill, and they both winced.

"Sun's coming up," she said. "Let's go in."

LINN TOSSED HER JACKET and purse on the hall table. What she wanted to do was fold herself into Kellan's arms and let herself realize that it was really over—or as over as it was going to get. Arroyo would be extradited and then she'd have a whole bunch of other things to worry about.

But right now she couldn't think that far into the future. Things weren't settled between herself and Kellan, and after tonight, she was taking no more chances. They hadn't been able to communicate during the worst moments, and she wasn't going to let another opportunity go by.

"Do you want a cup of coffee or something?" she asked.

"No, thanks."

"Juice? Breakfast?"

"No." He caught her around the waist. "I want to kiss you, take into the bedroom, look at you for a while, kiss you again and make love to you."

Linn smiled up at him. "Can you be more specific?"

It never failed to amaze her how fearless he was with words. But she was learning to be just as fearless with actions, so she did what she'd been wanting to do for hours. His big hands cradled her back, and she rubbed her cheek on his shoulder, feeling the heat and strength of his muscles under the pale-blue dress shirt he still wore. He must have left the suit jacket in his car.

"I like a man who knows what he wants," she murmured.

"There's more on the list. Want to hear it?"

"Can I do that lying down?"

"Absolutely."

She took his hand and led him into her bedroom.

"You know, I don't think I've ever been in here," he said, looking around him with interest. "Usually we don't get any farther than the couch. Nice parrots."

"That's a parrot and a chicken."

"Right. You told me that. Is that one of your mom's paintings?"

"The mate to the one in the living room. This one's called *Star Gazer.*"

He tilted his head. "Those are stars?"

"Never mind the art. We can talk about it later. Take your shirt off."

"Yes, ma'am."

She watched him pull the knot out of his tie and then slide the buttons through their holes one by one, revealing his chest a little at a time until the tie hung down on either side of the open placket. He might be in the advanced stages of exhaustion, but he was still the sexiest thing she'd ever laid eyes on.

He shrugged out of the shirt and she took a long breath of satisfaction.

"What?" he said.

"You. All I want to look at is you."

"I guess that makes us even. Much as I like those leather pants, I'm not sure I want to get into bed with them. Take 'em off."

"These are suede, I'll have you know." She unzipped them and brushed regretfully at the wine stain on the right thigh. "Not the best fashion choice for crawling around in the backs of trucks, I discovered."

He leaned back on the pillows. "It kind of went with the theme—you know, the woman in leather beating up the bad guy. An improvement on the red dress. Much more you."

"Great," she grumbled as she pulled the red tank top over her head. "I can just imagine what the team will make of *that*." She tossed the tank top on the chair by the window and crawled onto the coverlet next to him.

"The team thinks the same as I do," he murmured into her hair.

"What, that you need a whip and a chair to make love to me?" Intellectually she knew that this was the kind of backhanded compliment male investigators paid. Half mocking, half admiring, sometimes insulting. She should be used to it, but somehow she never quite managed.

She thought he might chuckle, but he didn't. "You don't miss much."

"I have ears."

Gently he pulled a tiny piece of adhesive from her skin, just beneath her bra. She must have missed it when she was peeling out of the transmitter earlier. He touched the reddened spot. "Did that hurt?"

"No."

He continued softly, "The good thing about it is the guys are too intimidated to make a pass at you. Which leaves the field clear for me."

"I've been meaning to talk to you about that."

"Do you have to keep your underwear on?"

"Yours is still on," she pointed out.

He stripped it off and tossed it on the floor, then watched her release the front catch of her red lace bra. He lifted the narrow straps off her shoulders with a finger and trailed it down her arm, as if tracing her bones.

"What would you think if I wrote the corporal's exam and transferred? I was thinking about organized crime or maybe the serial crimes unit."

She pushed up on one elbow in astonishment, and when his gaze didn't so much as flicker away from her own, she knew he had to be serious.

"But you love narcotics," was all she could think of to say. "You're so good at it."

"I'm so tired of it," he corrected her. "I've been doing it for three years, and this last six months has burned me out in a bad way. Yeah, I'm good at it, but so are you. So is Danny. Coop I'm not so sure of. I think his heart is in homicide, but he sticks here because he thinks asking for a transfer would be letting the team down. If I do it first, that frees him up." He paused. "Most important, it frees us."

She hardly dared ask, but she had to. If he could tell her exactly what he wanted, then she could, too. "Frees us to…?"

"To do this." He kissed her, softly, tenderly. "To stop sneaking around. To come out of the closet, as it were."

Because he would no longer be her boss. He would move on and leave the field clear for her own path to success.

To cover up her emotion, she quipped, "To tell Coop he won his bet?"

"You heard about that, too?" Then the crinkles around his eyes smoothed out, and he grew serious. "What do you think? Should I go for it?"

She knew what he was really asking, because it could only mean one thing. "You're thinking long-term, aren't you? For the two of us?"

He grinned. "You sound like a business proposal, but that's so you."

A business proposal? She'd show him a proposal. Her lashes drooped and she allowed a sultry pout to curve her lips. When he blinked, she knew she had his complete attention.

"I'm not thinking of business at all, darling. I'm thinking in terms of pleasure. Of fabulous sex. Of moving your king-size bed in here so you can look at my Mexican chicken every morning. I want you around full-time. I love you." She might have started off with Caroline's accent, but she said the final words as Linn.

Kellan cradled her face in one hand, his fingers soft on her skin.

"I've built a career on making deals," he said, smiling into her eyes, "but that's the best one I've ever heard."

His mouth came down on hers, and she forgot about proposals and propositions and everything but the way her desire flared up to meet his, the way her body curved to welcome his hands, the way she melted inside when he touched her.

And then she couldn't think at all.

"INVESTIGATOR NICHOLS, would you come in here, please?"

Linn looked up from the paperwork that lay scattered like unraked leaves all over the surface of her desk.

"Me, sir?" What had she done now, besides not get all these blasted forms filled out fast enough? Form 632—Incident Report. Form 632B—Exhibit List. Form 715—Felony Charge Report. Form 1470—

"Now, Investigator. If you don't mind."

"Right, sir. Sorry."

Linn followed Lieutenant Bryan into his office and halted on the threshold. Kellan sat in one of the two chairs in front of the desk, and smiled at her as Bryan sat in his big leather upholstered chair that he'd had brought in from a local furniture company on his own nickel.

Bryan folded his hands on the blotter and looked them over. "Good work on Arroyo, you two."

"Thanks, sir," Kellan said. "Any word?"

"The DEA is being close-lipped as usual, but rumor has it that they're going to extradite."

Kellan slapped the arm of his chair. "They can't do that! We've got him on felony importing, trafficking, fraud, you name it. I want to face that guy in court."

"Yeah, well, apparently the Colombian government is kicking up such a fuss that the governor is giving him back to them."

"We know and they know that he's got rich friends in the junta," Linn said. "The fuss is probably a smoke screen to set him free so he can go on doing business."

"Probably. The DEA is having a thing or two to say about it as we speak. But that's out of our hands. What's in our hands is this memo I have here from Internal Affairs."

Linn's stomach plunged, and her fingers turned icy cold.

"Saying what?" Kellan asked calmly, as if he could care less.

"Offering me a couple of suggestions on how I can run my shop."

Kellan and Linn sat in silence, waiting.

"Apparently they're concerned about the possibility of fraternization among the ranks. Improper behavior. Distraction."

"What evidence do they have for that, sir?" Linn asked through dry lips. Here it was. The end of her very bright but brief career with CLEU. After this, even Santa Rita PD would find it most entertaining when her application for re-employment came across the desk.

"They don't have any evidence," Bryan replied. If he'd been a smoking man, Linn was sure, he'd have been chewing his cigar. "They seem to think that just because I have a female investigator, I need to be vigilant about the behavior of my troops on State time." He held up the memo and glared at it. "Of course, nobody comes out and says so directly. It's all a bunch of bullshit about EEOC compliance and the harassment policy and the empowerment of underrepresented demographics. That would be you." He glanced at Linn over the top of the paper.

"Yes, sir," she said.

"So to avoid future problems of this sort, it's incumbent upon me to act."

Oh, God. She was going to be fired. She, the underrepresented demographic, had not only slept with Kellan Black, she'd admitted she was in love with him and proposed they live together. Now it was all over. The talk had spread outside the team to the other floors, and she was going to take the consequences.

"Investigator Black, let me be the first to congratulate you."

Kellan glanced at Linn, his eyes wide and confused. "On what, sir?"

"On your promotion from team lead to corporal. If you want it, that is." Bryan pulled a thicker sheet of paper—they had better stationery on the executive floor—from a file and handed it to him. "These are your test scores. You've been on the streets a long time, so it would be a big change for you if you decide to take it. Corporal isn't a total desk job, but there's enough time in a chair to make your butt as flat as mine."

"Thanks, sir." Kellan stared at the paper. "Geez. Ninety-two percent. How do you like that?"

The lieutenant turned to Linn. "Investigator Nichols, I've put in to have your probation period terminated."

For a moment Linn couldn't believe she'd heard the words. "Terminated, sir?" That was just like a male-dominated profession. Get a memo from Internal Affairs, get spooked, promote the guy and fire the woman.

Well, fine. She'd go to the EEOC and—

"Yes," Bryan confirmed. "Anybody who can take down Rick O'Reilly single-handed—with or without abusing alcohol—deserves full officer status, retroactive to the date of the arrest in July. With commensurate pay, of course."

Kellan grinned at her in a way that told her he'd had something to do with this. "I can't believe you tried to open a fifty-dollar bottle of merlot on Tricky Ricky's head. That's alcohol abuse in the extreme."

"Thanks," Linn managed. She would not cry. Absolutely not. "To both of you."

"Congratulations, Nichols, and welcome to the team. Black, take a little time to think about accepting your stripes. I just need to know your decision by Wednesday, so they get your rank right when I put in your names for commendations."

Linn sat back in the chair, feeling a little winded. There was just no end to all the surprises.

Bryan gazed from one to the other. "Whether we get to keep him or not, nailing Arroyo was a good piece of work. Creative, effective teamwork. You two put it on the line and succeeded. So I felt commendations were the least I could do. The rest of your careers are up to you." He pushed his chair back and stood, reaching over the desk to shake their hands. "Now, get out of here and go do something different and interesting. Like work." Bryan waved them out, but Linn could swear she saw a grin playing at the corners of his mouth.

Kellan walked her back to her cubicle. Out of the corner of her eye, Linn saw the heads of her teammates bobbing up and down over the tops of the cubes.

Uh-oh.

Her sense of self-preservation went on full alert. Even so, she wasn't quite prepared when she got back to her desk and saw what was sitting on her pile of paperwork.

The guys were all leaning on the tops of their cubes now. Kellan picked up the navy-blue baseball cap with Get a CLEU stitched in gold lettering on the front. He turned it over, and she saw that Coop, Danny, Kellan, and even Lieutenant Bryan had signed the beige underside of the bill.

"Investigator Nichols, since your probation is

over, it's my duty to welcome you officially to the team."

He jammed the cap on her hair and she smelled sulphur a split second before someone—Coop, she thought—tossed a string of firecrackers in her trash can, where they exploded in amplified abandon amid the whooping and applause of her team.

Kellan grabbed her and kissed her soundly, right there in front of everyone. But when he spoke, it was for her ears alone.

"And to the rest of my life," he said softly. "If you want it. It's up to you. Just as long as you know I love you."

She grabbed the cap to keep it from falling off and smiled up into his eyes. "Did I ever have a choice?"

Which—this time—wasn't such a bad thing.

# HARLEQUIN®
## Temptation
### is turning twenty!

**We're young, we're legal (well almost)
and we're old enough to get into trouble!**

And to celebrate our coming-of-age, we're
reintroducing one of our most popular miniseries.

Whenever you want a sassy, sexy book with
a little something out of the ordinary, look for...

## Editor's Choice

**Don't miss July's pick...**

# I SHOCKED THE SHERIFF
## by MARA FOX

When Roxy Adams shows up in her bright yellow Porsche,
Sheriff Luke Hermann knows he and his small Texas town will never
be the same. Within twenty-four hours, he's pulled her out of a catfight,
almost hauled her off to jail and spent the most incredible moments
of his life in her bed. But Luke knows she'll love him and leave him
soon enough. Still, before she does, he intends to make sure
she'll miss being held in the long arms of the law....

*Available wherever Harlequin books are sold.*

**www.eHarlequin.com**          HTECSTS

If you enjoyed what you just read,
then we've got an offer you can't resist!

# Take 2 bestselling
# love stories FREE!
# Plus get a FREE surprise gift!

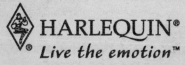

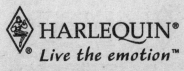

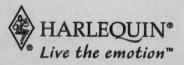